SUGAR CREEK GANG

THE
SWAMP ROBBER

Original title:
The Sugar Creek Gang

Paul Hutchens

MOODY PRESS • CHICAGO

THE SUGAR CREEK GANG
by Paul Hutchens

© Copyright, 1940, by
Wm. B. Eerdmans Publishing Company

Assigned to Paul Hutchens, 1965
Moody Press Edition, 1966

1

It was the laziest day I ever saw and so hot it would have made any boy want to go fishing or swimming—or maybe both. I don't think I was ever so glad in my life that school was out, 'cause just as soon as I saw those big fat fishing worms being turned up by Dad's plow when he was breaking the garden, I knew what I wanted to do. What I *had* to do, in fact, or the whole day would be spoiled.

Right away I laid my rake down—for I was raking the yard—and went out behind our garage to a whole barrelful of empty tin cans which we'd pretty soon have to haul away to the dump down along Sugar Creek. I picked out the best bait can I could find, threw in a handful of dirt, and started dropping in the biggest, juiciest fishing worms you ever saw—the kind that would make any fish go so crazy with hunger he'd risk getting caught rather than let the worm wriggle around on the hook all by itself. Like that time I sneaked into Mom's pantry and filled my pockets full of cookies and had my mouth full too just as Mom came hurrying down from upstairs where she'd been making the beds. Mom took one look at me, called out sharply, "William Jasper Collins!" and made a dive for me. She caught me too and—but that's a story I don't tell anybody about. Only after the licking quit hurting, I made up my mind I'd never take any more cookies without asking first.

I've got the best Mom in the world, don't think I haven't. I was just a little boy then and didn't know any better. But I guess that licking hurt Mom worse than it did me, 'cause long after I'd quit crying, I saw her eyes were kinda red around the lids. And that night when I'd said my prayers and been tucked into bed, she hugged me awful tight.

But as I said, that was when I was a little boy not more than seven years old. Now I say my prayers all by myself, climb into bed in the dark, and just call, "Good night!" down the stairs. I wouldn't let Mom know for the world that I kinda miss being tucked in, but I do just the same.

Well, pretty soon I had that bait can almost full of worms. I was thinking how hot it was here in the garden and how cool it would be down at the mouth of the branch and how Roy Gilbert and I would just lie there in the new green grass and watch the lazy specks of foam floating along on the water. And every now and then our bobbers would start acting funny, moving around in circles and ducking under the water like tiny diving birds, and our string of fish would get longer and longer with rock bass and chub and—

"*Jasper!*" Dad's big voice was just like a finger being poked into a great big beautiful soap bubble. It burst my dream all to nothing. And when Dad

4

called me Jasper instead of Bill, I knew he didn't like what I was doing.

I set the bait can down in the deep furrow and answered innocently, "What?"

"What are you up to?" Dad demanded. He had the horse's reins slipped around his shoulders, and his hands were gripping the plow handles real tight. I could tell 'cause his sleeves were rolled up, and the muscles on his arms were like great big ropes. My dad was awful strong—or maybe I should say *very* strong. My folks are having a hard time teaching me to use the right words. It's awful hard to quit using the wrong ones, you know.

I didn't know what to say to my dad. So I just called back indifferently, "Nothin' " and picked up a clod of dirt to throw at a blackbird that was gobbling up all the worms I had missed.

"Come here!" Dad said roughly, "and bring that can of worms with you!"

My heart went *flop*. I couldn't fool Dad in anything, and I knew better than to try. But I could see the whole day being spoiled. Just think of all those fish swimming around on the bottom of the creek hungry for nice wriggling worms. And just think of how Dad liked to eat fish when they were all cleaned and rolled in cornmeal and fried crisp and brown the way Mom can fry them. I decided to remind Dad how good fish would taste for supper that night while I picked up the can of worms and walked across the garden to where he was waiting for me. He could always read my mind just like I could read a book. I was in the fifth grade in school, you know.

Dad's big blackish-red eyebrows were down. He had turned around and was sitting on the cross piece between the plow handles. I was standing there holding the can of worms in both hands. The horses were so hot, white lather was all over them. They'd been sweating so much, that is, there was lather where the harness rubbed their sides, and you could smell the sweat. Sweat was trickling down Dad's face too. I guess there never was a hotter day in the spring with little heat waves dancing all over the garden.

I kept looking down at my toes which were digging themselves into the cool new-turned earth, and Dad kept glaring at my can of worms. I hadn't really done anything wrong, hadn't exactly planned or even thought anything wrong. Except maybe I was wishing I didn't have to rake the yard and hating rakes, hoes, garden-making, and all work. I guess you'd call it being lazy. Maybe it was.

"Well?" Dad demanded. Then I saw his snow-white teeth gleaming under his red-brown moustache and a twinkle in his eye. It was like a cool dive into Sugar Creek on a smothering hot day. Whenever I saw Dad's teeth shining under his moustache, I knew everything was all right.

"Bill Collins," he said, and I felt better than ever —even though his voice was still gruff. "I want you to take that garden rake, clean it off, and put it away in the toolhouse. Then get your long cane fishing pole and go down to the mouth of the branch—you and Roy Gilbert or some of the boys—and fish and fish and wade in the branch until you get over that terrible case of spring fever. And don't come back until you've caught all the fish that'll bite! You've had a hard school year—with your arithmetic, geography, and science—and you need a rest!"

At first I couldn't believe he meant it. But when he reached out, kinda put his arm around my shoulder, gave me half a hug, and said, "I was a boy once too," I believed him without trying. You should have seen me carry that long cane fishing pole in one hand and the can of worms in the other running straight toward the mouth of the branch where I knew Roy'd be waiting for me. For the night before we'd laid our plans to meet there at two o'clock if we could.

But I never dreamed so many things could happen all in one day, nor that before I'd get back home again Roy and I'd have been scared almost to death, nor that it was going to be the beginning of the most exciting week of my whole life.

2

IT HAPPENED THIS WAY. Roy and I were lying there in the grass on the bank of the creek just like I told you we would. Our fishing poles reached far out over the water, and funny-looking, enormous-eyed, four-winged dragonflies nosed around our lines like humming birds around Mom's morning glories back home. All of a sudden my bobber, which was nothing more than a big cork out of Mom's vinegar jug, started acting like it was alive. It moved around in a funny little half circle, kinda slow at first, and then *plunk!* just like that!—it ducked under, making a big splash. The end of my pole bent clear down and struck the water with a smack.

I knew before I could think that I'd hooked a big fish. I grabbed my end of the pole quicker than anything and held on tight. Roy told me afterward that my eyes stuck out like a dragonfly's when I was pulling that fish in. And my *line* didn't break either 'cause I had a brand new one. That's another reason why I knew my Dad liked me, maybe better'n any dad ever liked his boy before. When I'd gone to get my fishing pole out of the toolshed an hour before, it had had a brand new line on it with a reel and everything. Dad acted surprised when he saw it, but there was a twinkle in his gray eyes. And I knew he'd bought it for me.

Maybe you think I wasn't scared though when my bare feet slipped on the edge of the bank and flew right out from under me and I went down *kersplash* into the water, still holding onto that fishing pole for dear life. Roy was standing on the shore jumping up and down, yelling at the top of his lungs, and screaming at me what to do and not to let go the pole.

"I *saw* him!" he cried. "He was a big black bass two feet long!"

I could barely touch the bottom of the creek with my feet. While I was feeling the heavy pulling and jerking of that big fish on the end of the line and thinking about my new overalls being all wet and what Mom would say when I got home, Roy got hold of one of my hands and started to pull me out. "Give me the pole, quick!" he screamed. And then, just like it had happened to me, it happened to him too. His feet slipped and there we were, both of us in the water. Of course we could both swim so there wasn't any danger of drowning. You know, everybody ought to learn how to swim when he's little 'cause you can never tell when he'll either have to swim or drown.

Well, between the two of us we landed the fish. It was a big black bass all right, only it was about fourteen inches long—or maybe twelve—instead of two feet like Roy had said. And that's how he came

9

to get the nickname Dragonfly. His eyes were bigger than his head. Anyway, he was always seeing things twice as big as they were. He kinda liked the name and so did I. I felt quite proud that I'd thought of it first.

I tell you, that water felt good! "Now that we're all wet, we'd just as well go in swimming," Dragonfly said. "Besides, we'll have to let our clothes dry, won't we? And they'll dry quicker than anything hanging out on those bushes while we swim."

Dad hadn't told me I couldn't go swimming. I guess he figured maybe I'd like to, and he didn't want me to be tempted to disobey him and then have to have a licking. Dragonfly's parents hadn't told him not to either. So in about a minute and a half we had that twelve-inch bass—oh well, maybe he was only about eleven inches long—fastened on a stringer and swimming around in his jail over in the branch which empties into the creek right near where we'd been fishing. Our clothes were hanging on some bushes drying, and we were out there in that fine, clean water, splashing, swimming, diving, and having the time of our lives. Understand, we were waiting for our clothes to dry. We weren't just swimming for the fun of it, of course!

We stayed in maybe a half hour having a grand old time and wishing all the gang was there. Let me tell you about our gang, the finest bunch of boys you ever heard of. I reckon there never will be a gang of

10

boys in the whole world that'll have any more fun than we did. There was Little Jimmy Foote, who was the littlest one of us and who always obeyed his parents and was a sort of mascot for us 'cause he was so good. Anyway, he seemed to bring us good luck whenever he was along. We didn't care if he was about the most religious one of our gang 'cause he was so likeable. And he wasn't any sissy either! Say, that little fellow was brave! Once when there was a bear after us, and Little Jim was carrying Big Jim's rifle—but that's another part of my story which I can't tell you till a little later.

Well, there was Little Jim and Poetry and—but let me tell you about Leslie Thompson. We called him Poetry because he was always quoting a verse or two of poetry. Everything he saw would start him off and sometimes we'd have to shut him up or the rest of us wouldn't get a chance to say a word. He was fatter than anything, almost as broad as he was tall, and his voice was changing so that it sounded awful squawky. He used to sing soprano in the junior choir in our church, but now he wouldn't sing at all. And folks just don't seem to understand that when a boy's voice gets all squawky like a duck with a bad cold, he's terribly bashful about singing or talking in public. It didn't mean that Poetry was any less interested in church at all 'cause once I stayed all night at his house and we slept together. Before we went to bed he got right down on his knees and prayed first. And when he

11

got through saying his little poem prayer which he'd learned when he was little, he added a lot of words of his own just like he was talking to somebody right in the room. And I guess maybe he was. It kinda scared me at first, but I didn't let him see a stubborn old tear that got in my eyes about that time. Anyway, that's how I learned to add things to my prayer too.

Well, Poetry was always acting mysterious and was going to be a detective someday he said. And he was always getting into mischief.

And then there was Circus Browne whose real name was Daniel August Browne. Whatever his parents wanted to give him such a long-legged name for, I don't know. We called him Circus because he was so acrobatic. He could turn handsprings, walk on his hands, turn the pinwheel and he could shin up a tree quicker'n anybody I ever saw.

Besides Dragonfly, Poetry, Little Jim, Circus, and me, there was Big Jim. We called him Big Jim 'cause he and Little Jim had the same names and we didn't want to get them mixed up. Big Jim was the leader of the gang and he knew all the things a leader ought to know. He'd belonged to a boy scout patrol once before he'd moved into our neighborhood and was what they call a first class scout. First he'd been a tenderfoot, then a second class, then a first class. He could have gone on to qualify for star or life or eagle rank, but his folks had had to move and there wasn't any scout troop where we lived. Besides, you have to be twelve years old to be even a tenderfoot. So that would have meant that Dragonfly, Poetry, Little Jim, and I would have been left out. So Big Jim just called us The Gang.

Say, Big Jim was strong, almost as strong as my Dad, I reckon, and he used almost perfect English. He knew exactly what to do in case anybody fainted. He could make a tourniquet for stopping the flow of blood when anybody was bleeding terribly. He could tie twenty-one different kinds of knots, such as the Magnus hitch, the fisherman's bend, the half hitch, and the bowline knot. He was the catcher of our ball team and could knock more home runs than any of us. He could jump the farthest and was the best fighter I ever saw. Only we didn't get into many fights on account of Big Jim kept other boys in the neighborhood from starting anything, they being scared of him.

Poetry could quote more poetry than any of us. Circus could climb a tree the fastest and do more acrobatic stunts. Dragonfly was able to see bigger things and see the farthest. And Little Jim was more of a Christian than the whole lot of us put together. As for me, I guess I was just an ordinary boy. I didn't even have a nickname except just plain Bill, which is short for William.

As I said, Dragonfly and I must have stayed in the water about a half hour. Anyway, when you haven't been in swimming for a long time and it's such a terribly hot day, time goes pretty fast and you forget about everything else except how much fun you're having.

It was Dragonfly who saw it first—saw *him*, rather. All of a sudden Dragonfly stopped splashing and yelling, and hissed to me, "Quick, Bill! Get down under the water! Somebody's comin'!"

We both dropped down so only our chins and noses were sticking out, looking maybe like a couple of turtles with only their noses showing above the water.

"Look!" Dragonfly whispered. "It's an old man with long white whiskers, and he's coming right straight this way!"

"I don't see anything," I said. And then I saw him: a short, fat man about as big around as a barrel, bareheaded, with whiskers and long shaggy, white hair that reached clear down to his belt. Only he didn't have on any belt on account of he was wearing a pair of old overalls. He had on dark glasses and he shuffled along like he couldn't see very well. He looked just like an old tramp. "Itinerants" Dad called them, which didn't sound so bad. But I guess there never was a boy that wasn't a little bit scared of one of them, especially one that looked as fierce as that one did.

3

WE KEPT AS QUIET as we could, hoping the old man wouldn't see us and would go right on past. We didn't want him to take our fishing poles or our big bass or—

"Look!" Dragonfly pinched me so hard under the water that I nearly yelled. But the fact is I was so scared I couldn't have yelled very loud, for I'd never seen such a fierce-looking man in my life.

"He's spied our clothes!" Dragonfly said. Sure enough he had, and he was pushing his way through the tall weeds right straight toward them.

We knew right then we'd better do something quick, for I had a brand new knife in my overall pocket, and Dragonfly had a watch in his.

"Let's scream like a hundred wild Indians," Dragonfly said, his teeth chattering. It sounded like a good idea, so we both let out a yell as loud as we could, making it sound as fierce as if we were a whole tribe of Indians. Only I knew it must have sounded like two kids, half scared to death, which it did.

But the old man acted like he was deaf or something, for he didn't even look around. He was standing right near where our clothes were hanging, and in a second he was going through our pockets. He found Dragonfly's watch first and held it up in the sunlight close to his big dark glasses, brushed it against his long, white whiskers like he was brushing dust off of it, put it to his ear and listened, then shook his head as if he couldn't hear a thing.

"My—my *watch!*" Dragonfly whispered and gulped. I'd never seen him so scared before. And being scared is kinda like getting the measles—it's catching. Dragonfly's face made me afraid too. But if getting scared is contagious, so is getting angry. Pretty soon we were both so mad we knew we were going to do something fierce in just about a minute.

We yelled again, a wild, blood-curdling scream. But do you think that made any difference? Not a bit!

"He's deaf!" Dragonfly said. I believed it. And when I saw my new knife going down that old man's pocket, I began to get madder than ever. Then the old man just naturally picked up our clothes, slung them over his shoulder, and waddled back through the tall grass and weeds whistling. *Whistling,* mind you!

We knew we couldn't go home without our clothes, only at that time I didn't know much of anything, I was so mad.

And so was Dragonfly. We knew we would have to do something, and you can bet your life we did. We climbed up that creek bank, picked up a couple of clubs, and whooped it up like a whole tribe of Indians swinging our clubs and yelling, "Come back here with our clothes! Stop or we'll shoot!" and about everything frightening we could think of.

But that big round barrel of a man, with his long white hair shining in the sunlight, just turned around and glared at us. He seemed to know the lay of the land there too, for he shuffled quickly to the right and tossed our clothes right over into the middle of a brier patch and said gruffly, "Help yourself!" *Brier patch*, mind you! And both of us barefoot and stark naked! Why we'd be scratched half to death trying to get those clothes!

That was too much. We both made a dive for him, and before you could say Jack Robinson we'd caught up with him—not because we could run faster, for he was faster'n a deer, but because he stumbled and fell and rolled down the hill. We stumbled over him, landing right on top of him, and getting our arms and legs all tangled up like an octopus doing an acrobatic stunt.

"Stop!" he cried, "don't hurt me! I'll give up!" And then, as if he was crazy, he started quoting poetry:

> "Jack and Jill went up the hill
>   To fetch a pail of water;
> Jack fell down and broke his crown,
>   And Jill came tumbling after."

In a jiffy those long whiskers were off, and the long hair, and dark glasses. And we were looking straight into the mischievous blue eyes of Leslie Poetry

17

Thompson who started to laugh and laugh as loud as he could and quoted from "The Night Before Chrismas":

"He had a broad face and a little round belly,
That shook when he laughed, like a bowl full
of jelly."

Poetry sprang to his feet and began to dance a jig and to sing:

"Hey, diddle, diddle,
The cat and the fiddle,
The cow jumped over the moon.
The little dog laughed
To see such sport,
And the dish ran away with the spoon."

He held up Dragonfly's watch and my knife and started all over again about the cat and the fiddle.

Well I was still mad and so was Dragonfly. And as much as we liked good old mischievous Poetry, we made him wade out into that brier patch and get our clothes which were still a little wet. Then we all went in swimming. Poetry got ducked again and again for being so smart. Only it was just like trying to duck a rubber barrel; he wouldn't stay under, and he could swim and dive like a fish.

"Where'd you get your whiskers?" I asked when we were dressing.

"And your dark glasses and your long hair?" Dragonfly added.

"Wouldn't you like to know?" Poetry asked. Then he lowered his voice and looked around mysteriously. "I found 'em," he said.

"Found 'em?" Dragonfly and I asked in chorus.

"In the old hollow sycamore tree down along the swamp."

"How do you suppose they got there?" I asked.

Poetry looked at me scornfully as if I was too ignorant to know much about mysterious things. "They grew there, just like moss," he said.

"Maybe there's some robber or something around here," Dragonfly said, trying on the dark glasses.

Poetry looked pretty serious when Dragonfly said that. And that, too, was like getting the measles. The more we thought about it, the more we began to wonder if Dragonfly might not be right. That old sycamore tree was the biggest tree around here anywhere —the biggest around, anyway. And about three or four feet from the ground was a big opening. And inside it was all hollow, large enough for three of us boys to stand in it at the same time, that is, three the size of Little Jim and Dragonfly and me.

Poetry just about filled it himself. In fact, he was so fat this year he couldn't even get inside the opening. The tree grew about fifteen feet from a steep precipice that dropped straight down a rocky bank to Sugar Creek. It was an awful lonely place down in that part of the woods, and none of us boys ever went there alone 'cause our folks didn't want us to. But we sometimes went there together.

Somebody'd started the rumor that that old swamp was haunted, and that meant ghosts. While none of us boys believed in ghosts, we weren't exactly hoping to meet one without Big Jim along who could have made short work of any ghost in a jiffy, he was so strong. But Poetry! You couldn't ever tell what he was going to do next. And as I told you, he'd already made up his mind he was going to be a detective when he grew up, and he wasn't afraid of anything.

The three of us sat there looking pretty sober-faced, talking about what we'd better do. Each of us tried on the disguise just to see how we looked with it on. Then all of a sudden it was five o'clock and we knew we'd better be getting home quick or our folks'd be worrying about us. That was one of Big Jim's rules: We weren't to cause our parents any worry if we could help it.

Dragonfly made me take the fish even though we had both caught it. Tomorrow, we decided, we'd get Big Jim and Circus and Little Jim and the six of us would go down along the swamp and investigate that old hollow tree. We'd sneak up on the place and attack it from ambush. 'Course there wasn't anything to it, but you never could tell.

4

IT FELT MIGHTY GOOD to be carrying that big fish home for Dad to see although I kept wondering what Mom would say about my wrinkled overalls. They were pressed so nicely when I'd gone away.

But Mom was as good a mother as Dad was a father. She was standing in the kitchen doorway when I came up past the barn and the garden carrying my big black bass, the fishing pole, and the bait can. Dad was washing his face and hands in a big wash basin under our grape arbor which ran along the side of the garage. He straightened up with soap suds all over his face and neck and looked me over from head to foot. Then his eyes lit up proudly while I held up the fish for him to see. Dad was looking at the fish and Mom was looking at my soiled overalls.

"It's wonderful," Dad said.

"They're terrible," Mom said.

I didn't have a chance to be either glad or sad, now did I? But I was worried some just the same, 'cause I didn't want to make Mom feel bad.

"I'll wash them myself," I said to Mom.

"He won't need washing," Dad said, "only cleaning and skinning"—meaning the fish, of course, not me.

Just then the telephone rang and Mom had to go answer it, so I had a minute to be happy about my big fish. Dad brought a ruler and measured it. "Ten and one-half inches," he said. And he gave me the other half of that hug he'd started to give me earlier in the afternoon.

Right away supper was ready. Soon as I had washed my face and hands and combed my hair—I wet my hair a lot too before I combed it so it wouldn't look like I'd gotten it wet going in swimming—we sat down to supper. I was still feeling kinda heavy around the heart on account of my overalls, even though I was as cheerful as anything on the outside and as hungry as a bear on the inside.

Mom's big soft brown eyes kept watching me all the time. We all bowed our heads quietly before eating. Hungry as I was, I kept my eyes shut all the time Dad was praying, which wasn't very long. Dad knew how hungry a boy could get at mealtime, and most anytime. He was a boy once himself. Oh, Dad was a real Christian all right. I knew that not only 'cause he prayed and read the Bible and went to church but because he acted like one toward Mom and me and everybody else.

I was just itching to tell them the whole story about how I caught the fish, that is, how Drangonfly and I caught it. But I couldn't on account of not wanting Mom to know I fell in the creek. But pretty soon when Mom was waiting on the table and was pouring a second glass of milk for me, she reached down and kissed the top of my head just like I was a little boy. And she whispered in my ear, "Don't worry, Billy Boy, I know you didn't do it on purpose." Then she went around to her chair and sat down again. After that it was the easiest thing in the world to talk.

Dad laughed and laughed and wiped his eyes over me and Dragonfly falling into the water.

That night after I'd scrubbed my feet good and gone up to bed, calling, "Good night" at the top of the stairs, I stood beside my bed a long time before getting down on my knees to say my prayers. I looked out the window at the moonlight shining on the barn and the garage and the new garden. I could even see the little green tops of onion sets in long rows across the garden. Then I looked up at the Milky Way stretched like a big white bow across the sky and at all the thousands of stars. And I just kinda felt that God had made them, and I couldn't help but be glad I had a real Dad and Mom who loved Him and tried to teach me about Him. Somehow I couldn't help but think maybe He was like my mother and father, only more wonderful and a lot greater. He had made an awful pretty world, and He must have liked boys a lot 'cause He'd sent His own Son down to earth to be a boy Himself once.

I knelt down and said my little poem prayer and then added some words of my own which I can't remember now. I felt just like telling Jesus I loved

Him like I did my parents and maybe even more, but I was scared to. But I did love Him just the same. And I guess He can hear a boy's thoughts anyway, the same as his words. Only it's better to use real words when you can.

I tell you that nice clean bed felt good even if it was hot. The pillow was so big and soft, only—only—why it was wet! No, not much, but like someone had sprinkled a few drops of water on it.

And that's how I found out I'd been crying a little bit. I hadn't known it at all. I sighed a great big happy sigh, and the next thing I knew it was morning.

5

SAY, that was the finest morning you ever saw. The big red sun was just peeping up over the horizon like he wasn't quite awake yet and hated to get up. The birds were singing like everything. Right up in the top of our big walnut tree, which grew on the other side of the garden and where we had the biggest swing in the whole neighborhood and where the gang liked to play, was a robin hollering for all he was worth, "Jasper Collins! Get up, get up!" I liked robins though, even if they did call me Jasper.

And down on the ground, with his head cocked on one side listening for a worm or something, was another robin with his red breast in the sunlight. He must have seen a worm all right, for all of a sudden he turned like a flash and was pulling at something with his big black and yellow bill. And, sure enough, in a second there was a big long fishing worm in his mouth, twisting and squirming like it was on a hook.

You know, it really doesn't hurt fishing worms to be put on a hook, Dad said once. Dad is a sort of scientist-farmer, and he said something about it being just a "minor irritation" or something, which means it doesn't hurt much. Kinda like a boy getting his neck and ears washed with soap and water when he'd rather wash them himself by swimming and diving in Sugar Creek.

Pretty soon that robin flew up into a fork of the walnut tree where there was a whole nest full of little quintuplets waiting for their breakfast. Think of eating worms for breakfast! *Worms!*

I dressed in a hurry 'cause today was to be the big day. Right after dinner the gang would all get together, and Poetry would tell us what he'd found in the hollow tree down by the haunted swamp. We'd all arm ourselves with bows and arrows and slingshots and with a big club for Little Jim, and the fun would begin.

First thing, though, was getting through the morning, which would be awful long 'cause all of us boys helped our folks in the morning. That was Big Jim's rule. I guess there never was a boy that liked to work unless he could imagine his work was play. But Mom had been trying to teach me ever since I was little that work came first and then play. I guess she was right. Then, too, if you really love your parents, you like to do things that make them happy.

I helped Mom wipe the dishes, which most boys think is a girl's job, but it isn't when you don't have any girls in the family. I finished raking the lawn, built a fire, burned all the dead grass and leaves, and gathered up all the tin cans and things that somehow had gotten scattered all over the barnyard mainly 'cause I'd been using 'em for imaginary golf balls. I dropped the potato slices with the eyes in them into the long deep rows Dad had made across the garden and stepped on them with my bare feet so they'd be pressed down into the dirt better and would grow quicker. Maybe you think that wasn't fun, feeling the cool, damp dirt oozing up between my toes!

Pretty soon it was dinner time, and we had fish for dinner. "What kind of bait did you use to catch this bass?" Dad asked. And I said, between mouthfuls, having a hard time to eat slow on account of having to meet the gang at one o'clock, "Why, just plain worms. Why?"

"I just wondered," Dad said. "I found a nice little chub on the inside of him"—a chub is a small carp-like fish, you know—"and the little chub was full of fishing worms," Dad added.

I looked up surprised. That meant that first I'd hooked a little chub, and then the big bass had come along and had swallowed the chub. Right away I knew what kind of bait to use for bass the next time I wanted to catch one.

"It'll be all right to fish for bass today," Dad said, looking at Mom and winking. "You won't run any risk getting arrested."

"What?" I said, kinda scared.

"The bass fishing season opens today," Dad said. "If the game warden had seen you catch that one yesterday, it would have been too bad."

Well at ten minutes to one I was ready to go down to the spring where the gang had agreed to meet. It was Thursday, and we always met there on Thursday afternoons at one o'clock if we could.

I ran upstairs to get my binoculars thinking maybe we'd need them. On the way down again I stopped to fasten the strap around my neck, and all of a sudden I went numb all over. Pop had the radio going, listening to the afternoon news, and just that minute I heard the announcer say, ". . . warned to be on the lookout for a man suspected of being an accomplice in a bank holdup. It is believed he is hiding somewhere in the swamp—" I couldn't make out where 'cause there was a lot of static. . . . "He's described as having black hair and eyes and . . . ."

When I got downstairs and looked at myself in the mirror I was as white as a sheet. But I hurried out of doors quickly so the folks wouldn't see me and ran as fast as I could through the woods toward the spring. My heart beat wildly because of what I'd heard and because it looked like maybe we were going to have a chance to help catch a real robber.

6

I WAS THE FIRST ONE of the gang to get to the spring
and Circus was the last. He had a hard time persuad-
ing his parents how important it was not to miss a
meeting. Circus' folks—his dad especially—never did
understand boys very well, although his dad must have
been a boy once himself. But grown-up people are
funny in that way. They kinda forget that inside a boy
there is something that just makes him want to keep
his promise to the gang. And I tell you, it's pretty hard
to give in and obey your parents when they don't understand. But we had to, though. Big Jim said he'd
read it in the Bible as plain as day, *"Children, obey
your parents!"* Little Jim, who wasn't any relation to
Big Jim at all—only he had the same name—said
it was true 'cause he saw it in the Bible with his own
eyes. "Besides," Big Jim said, "if you ever want to
become a boy scout, one of the qualifications is obe-
dience."

Well, pretty soon we were all there. Big Jim had
a mysterious package under his arm. Circus climbed
a small elm sapling almost as soon as he got there
and was swaying in the top, back and forth, and looking every bit like a monkey in the zoo. Dragonfly
and Poetry and Little Jim and I started tumbling

around in the grass like kittens having a good time. All six of us boys were as tickled to see each other as if we hadn't been together in years.

The spring, you know, comes bubbling up out of a hole in a rock at the bottom of a steep, hill, only about twenty feet from the creek. Dad had had the water tested to see if it was all right, and it was.

Just that minute a big green shitepoke came flying up the creek with his long neck sticking out in front of him like the long handle on my green coaster wagon. His wings were flapping and driving him through the air awful fast. A shitepoke is a real green heron Dad says, but it's the most idiotic looking bird you ever saw.

I had just gotten my binoculars focused on him and was following him up the creek with my eyes when Poetry was reminded of a verse from *Hiawatha*. Away he went in his squawky voice which was about as squawky as the big quoke heron's which goes quoking up the creek at night sounding like a young rooster learning to crow:

> "Then the Little Hiawatha
> Learned of every bird its language,
> Learned their names and all their secrets;
> How they built their nests in summer,
> How they hid themselves in winter;
> Talked with them whene'er he met them,
> Called them Hiawatha's chickens."

Poetry finished the first verse and started the second when something came swinging down from up above and landed right on top of him. Circus had caught hold of the top of the elm sapling where he was sitting and swung himself out. The top of that tree had bent right over to the ground and brought him down with it. When he let go, the tree top flew right back up again. In another minute we were all trying it, each one climbing a tree and swinging from one to another or down to the ground, whichever we wanted to do. You can do that with elm trees, you know.

But all this was just wasting time, so pretty soon Poetry looked at me and I looked at him. We decided to ask Big Jim to call a meeting so he could show us what he'd found yesterday.

First though, Big Jim opened his package, and there was a whole packet of paper drinking cups. We knew right away what they were for 'cause we'd studied in school about how everyone ought to have individual drinking cups for health reasons.

Big Jim picked up the old rusty cup that was standing there on the rock and which everybody in the country had used for years maybe. We all stood solemn-like wondering what he was going to do. First he held it up for us to see and then he said dramatically, making a play out of it, "You can never tell when someone is going to drink out of it—someone who has some terrible disease maybe—and when the next person who uses the cup may become infected."

Then Big Jim set the cup down on the rock, and with another rock he pounded and hammered it until he'd smashed it all flat. Then he tossed it into the weeds, and pretty soon we had a sign up which said, "Please use paper drinking cups." When we were finished, those cups were fastened up on a tree by the spring in a little tin container just like you see in the cities, in street cars, or in most any public place.

All of a sudden Poetry was gone, and then a minute later he came hobbling down the hill like an old man with a long beard and long white hair and with dark glasses on. Dragonfly pinched me on the arm so hard I couldn't help but say, "Ouch," and then I shut up like a clam.

"Howdy boys," Poetry said in the quavery voice of an old man. "Do you reckon maybe a feller can get a drink of water at the spring here?"

Little Jim looked as white as a sheet for a minute. Circus' monkey face was as sober as a funeral. Dragonfly and I were holding our hands over our mouths to keep from laughing. I thought even Big Jim looked a little bit worried, for he was a boy even if he was our leader. He wasn't so much bigger than Poetry, at that.

"Where's my old rusty tin cup?" Poetry's voice quavered, and it didn't sound any more like Poetry than anything. But Circus saw his bare feet and noticed how fat he was, and a second later Poetry was standing bareheaded and looking surprised and disgusted. And Circus was already trying the disguise on himself to see how he would look.

Well, Big Jim called a meeting, and Poetry, Dragonfly, and I told them everything we knew, even to the radio announcement. Big Jim took it all pretty calmly, but I could see he was as much excited on the inside as the rest of us.

"Maybe I'd better run home and ask Mother if I can go," Little Jim said.

"Not much, you don't!" Circus said. "It's going to be a secret! 'Course if you're afraid—"

"I'm *not* afraid!" Little Jim shouted bravely.

'Course he *was* afraid and so were all of us, but a boy likes to be scared a little bit. It feels good.

So pretty soon we were there, right down along the swamp, walking cautiously toward the old hollow sycamore tree.

7

It was dragonfly who saw the man first, for as I told you before, he had the sharpest eyes of any of us.

"Phsst!" he hissed. "There's a funny looking man!" He dropped flat on the ground, which was a signal for all of us to do the same thing. It didn't do Poetry much good to lie down 'cause anybody couldn't help but see him, although maybe they wouldn't think he was a human being, but a big fat steer or a horse or something.

Sure enough there was a man all right about twenty yards from the tree and walking straight toward it— or rather he was just walking along kinda lazy-like but going toward the tree just the same, and he was whistling some kind of tune which sounded like "Old Black Joe."

Big Jim turned his face round toward us, raised his fingers to his lips and said, "Sh!" And his eyes said, "Don't you dare make a noise, any of you!" Then he handed the binoculars to me. I noticed particularly that the man looked awful young to be a bank robber, and he had coal black hair.

When we'd all had a look with the binoculars, we knew that something was really mysterious for the man was digging around in the old tree. "He's looking for something," Poetry couldn't help but say, thinking maybe of the whiskers and the glasses and the wig. It's a good thing the grass was tall where we were or the man might have seen us. Once he stopped what he was doing and looked around quick as if he'd heard something, then he went on whistling "Old Black Joe" and walked away, following the creek. Something must have scared him, for pretty soon he started to run for all he was worth.

I guess we lay there for maybe five minutes waiting for Big Jim to say we could get up. We could see from the expression on his face that he was thinking hard. Pretty soon he said, "It won't do for us to act like we know anything special. Let's just get up and be natural like a bunch of boys having a good time."

Circus was about the only one of us that didn't have any trouble acting natural when he was trying to. He yawned, stretched and said, "Boy, it feels good to lie here in the shade." Only there wasn't any shade there at all except what Poetry made, he being so awful fat.

So with all of us acting natural, or nearly so, we just moved along gang fashion until we got to the tree. Big Jim made us all stand back and keep on trying to act natural, which was pretty hard to do. We could hear him digging around in the tree with Little Jim's stick. Pretty soon he let out a low whistle and I saw him shove something into his pocket and keep right on digging around.

There was a queer look on his face when he came

back to where we were. Then all of a sudden there was a shot up the creek. Then another. And another!

It didn't take us long to get back to the spring, I can tell you, for that look in Big Jim's face and those gun shots scared us plenty. We were all so excited we could hardly talk, which was all right 'cause we were supposed to do nothing but run anyway, which we did.

At the spring, Big Jim took out of his pocket a dirty brown envelope and started to open it, when we all jumped suddenly like we were shot. We could hear footsteps coming, up along the top of the hill.

We all sat there so tense we couldn't move. Big Jim shoved the envelope in his pocket and started whistling. Poetry rolled over on his side, yawned and said, "Boy, I'm sleepy:

> In winter, I get up at night,
> And dress by yellow candle light;
> In summer, quite the other way
> I have to go to bed by day."

Little Jim sidled over to Big Jim, and his right hand crept into his so he wouldn't feel so scared. Circus and Dragonfly started a wrestling match, and I got my binoculars and focused them on a snake which was swimming along the creek.

The snake must have seen or heard us, for he ducked under the water and didn't come up again until he was almost all the way across and about ten feet farther down the creek.

All this time we knew the footsteps were coming nearer, even though we couldn't hear them.

I guess we were all pretty relieved when we looked up and saw it was my dad with a big pail in his hand coming for spring water. He stood looking at us, at our sign on the tree and at the paper drinking cups. Then he filled his pail and said casual-like, "You'd better come home at five-thirty tonight, Bill. This is Thursday, you know."

You see, Thursday night is prayer meeting night in our church. Some kids might think it's kind of goofy to go to prayer meeting, but I didn't 'cause I'd been going ever since I was old enough to be carried there. And when you've got a mother and father like mine, you think prayer meeting on Thursday night is all right. In fact, I felt sorry for Circus' folks who didn't go any place on Thursday nights except to places where they shouldn't—Circus' dad especially. He was always getting drunk. Circus' mom was really a good mother, but she didn't have a chance with so many children and all of them girls but one. Circus' folks didn't know anything at all about the Bible. It didn't seem fair for a boy to have that kind of parents, but that's the kind Circus had. All he knew about things like that was what he'd learned from Little Jim and Poetry and me, but mostly from Little Jim. Circus had already quit swearing because Little Jim didn't like to hear it. Circus was the only one of our gang that did swear. Big Jim wouldn't stand for it. So as quick as he knew it was wrong, he quit.

Well, just as my dad reached the top of the hill with his pail of water, he turned around and said without even being excited, "Maybe you boys would be interested to know that about twenty minutes ago the sheriff caught a boy bank robber down along the swamp. The robber is on his way to jail now. To the hospital first to get well of his wounds—They had to shoot him."

Little Jim looked kinda pale. I knew right away he was thinking about that robber, for pretty soon when Dad was gone he said, "I hope he doesn't die without being sorry. Mother says unless a man repents of his sin and lets Jesus come into his heart before he dies, he won't *ever* be saved and can't go to heaven at all!"

After Little Jim said that we all kept still for a minute, thinking different things. I wondered whether the bank robber's mother would go to jail to see him. How awful it would make her feel to have that kind of a boy. I wished every boy in the world had a mother like mine or Little Jim's or Poetry's. I bet there wouldn't be many bad boys in the world if they did have, would there?

We decided we'd better find a more secluded place than the spring before we opened that brown envelope 'cause at the spring you can never tell when somebody's going to come for a drink. So we climbed up on top of a high hill over on the east side of the woods to a big rock where we sometimes had our meetings. And in a few minutes we were all there looking at a rough drawing of some kind with scrawly writing on it.

Right in the middle of the page was a bed that looked like a hospital cot, and in the bed was an old man with a nurse standing there with a glass of water. The old man was saying, "More, please." Alongside the bed was a funny, crooked line, twisting along like a snake, and a little bird was in a tree close by singing, "Sweet, sweet, sweet." There were letters and numbers and other lines running off from the one that looked like a snake.

"It doesn't make sense!" Poetry exclaimed. It looked like he was right.

I kept watching Big Jim's face, for I knew he was thinking. Say, Big Jim had the kindest face you ever saw, with clear blue eyes and a chin that had a great big dimple right in the middle. There wasn't any sense to my noticing the yellow and black fuzz on his upper lip when I should have been thinking about the map, or whatever it was supposed to be, unless it was because some people call other people's faces "maps." Anyway, I thought that Big Jim was old enough, almost, to begin shaving and I kinda envied him being that old. For that little moustache meant that Big

Jim was almost a man. I guess every boy can hardly wait until he gets to be a man.

It was Dragonfly who saw it first, and in a jiffy he was jumping up and down and hollering for all he was worth, "I've got it! I've got it!"

Big Jim shut him up quick; all of us did, in fact. "Look!" Dragonfly said, "that nurse standing there means the old man is sick! He's asking for more water, and—and if you put *sick* and *more* together, you have *sycamore!* It stands for that old tree!"

I guess we were all pretty excited right that minute, and we must have made a lot of noise 'cause Big Jim said, "Calm down!" Now that Dragonfly'd seen it, it was as plain as day to the rest of us.

"And—and—and—," Dragonfly stuttered, "that snake crawling is a creek. And the bird singing, 'Sweet, sweet, sweet,' means *Sugar Creek!*"

It was just like fitting together a jigsaw puzzle, figuring out that map. Only it was harder. We were all sitting there on the rock with the map spread out between us, racking our brains to decide what the funny lines and words meant. From the tree there was an arrow with the number 20 written on it pointing straight east—that is, if the directions on the map were the same as those on any ordinary map. On the end of the arrow was the word *China,* and that didn't make any sense. Not until Little Jim said, kinda quiet-like as if he was afraid somebody'd make fun of his idea, "My daddy's brother is a missionary in China, and Daddy says China's right straight down through the center of the earth." Without knowing it, he had solved the puzzle for us, for that meant go twenty feet east and dig straight down and there we'd find whatever it was—the money, maybe—which had been stolen from the bank.

We all jumped up and started toward the sycamore tree with Big Jim in the lead. Having to go slow because Little Jim couldn't run as fast as the rest of us, we got there in about six minutes or a little more.

Well, there we were without a ruler or a tapeline, so how could we know how far twenty feet or twenty yards were without something to measure with! We weren't nearly as scared as we had been when we were there the first time 'cause we knew the robber'd been caught. But we were plenty excited, though.

"Somebody'll have to run home for a ruler or a tapeline," Big Jim said. We all looked at each other. None of us wanted to go knowing it was so near suppertime that whoever went might not get to come back. His folks might not understand how important it was, and he couldn't tell them.

"Let's roll Poetry over seven times, and that'll make twenty-one feet 'cause he's just three feet round," Circus suggested. Poetry turned red and gave Circus a savage look. "I'm thirty-five inches," he said disgustedly, "and you wouldn't know your arithmetic well enough to divide twenty feet by thirty-five inches."

"Maybe if he'd drink a pint of water," Dragonfly

suggested, "he'd be exactly three feet, and three times seven is twenty-one. Then we could measure back the length of his foot which is just twelve inches, and we'd find the right place." And Poetry looked more disgusted than ever. He was especially ashamed of having such long feet but he couldn't help it.

"I'm just four feet tall," Little Jim said. In a jiffy he was lying down with his feet against the sycamore tree and with his body pointing straight east. Well, that looked like a good idea, so we just used Little Jim for a measuring stick. Pretty soon we were what was supposed to be twenty feet from the tree. Poetry lay down and rolled over seven times too just to show he was a good sport and there wasn't much difference between the two measurements.

But we knew we'd figured wrong, for all around there the grass was fresh and green, and nobody had ever buried anything there unless it was a long time ago. So maybe the map meant twenty yards instead of twenty feet. Big Jim looked at his watch, then at me, and said, "It's five-thirty. We'll all have to go home to supper."

Of course we felt pretty disappointed, but we agreed to meet again the next afternoon at one o'clock if we could. Big Jim would bring a long fifty-foot tapeline, his father being a carpenter.

"I'll bring a gunnysack to put the money in," Little Jim volunteered. But we didn't laugh at him 'cause sometimes his ideas turned out to be all right.

8

MAYBE I NEVER TOLD YOU that Poetry was my very best friend, but he was. When I got home and had helped Dad with the chores and we were eating supper, the phone rang. It was Poetry's parents saying if we'd like to we could ride to church with them in their new car. I was glad 'cause that meant Poetry and I could sit together in church, that is, if we'd promise to be good and not get into mischief. But it would be a hard promise for any boy to keep—especially if he was sitting beside Poetry—even in church. His being mischievous didn't mean he was a bad boy, though, 'cause I knew he wasn't. Some boys are made different than others, I guess, and Poetry was that kind.

Right after supper Dad had me drive the cows down the lane to the pasture. "Be sure to shut the gate and hook it good and tight," he called to me just as I left the barnyard driving our five big Holstein milk cows.

"I will," I called back. With a long stick, which I always used when I was driving the cows, I trudged along happily thinking about tomorrow and wondering what we'd find, or if the map had been drawn by some crazy person and didn't have anything to do with the bank robbery at all. That was about the oldest and dirtiest envelope I'd ever seen, and the map looked like it had been drawn a hundred years ago—well, twenty years ago anyway, or maybe ten.

Pretty soon I heard Mom's voice calling me to hurry or we'd be late for church. When I got up close to the house I heard her complain a little to Dad, saying, "Whatever makes that boy so *irresponsible?*" or some such long word.

And Dad said, "He's a dreamer. He'll be all right if we give him time."

Well, pretty soon Poetry was there, and we were all in their car going up the road lickety-sizzle toward our church, which was maybe two miles from where we lived. You know we boys all lived out in the country in about the prettiest spot in the world, I reckon. Right across the road from our church, which was a country church, was a three-room schoolhouse. It wasn't the school we all went to 'cause we had a little one-room school of our own right in our neighborhood.

It didn't take us long to get there. It wasn't even dark yet, and our car was the first one to drive up in the big wide church yard and park. Soon people came from all directions, and the service began.

Poetry and I held the songbook together, and I noticed he didn't look at the page more'n half the time. He just growled along, singing a sort of bass, knowing most of the words from memory, he liked poetry so well.

The meeting wasn't exactly the kind to appeal to

real red-blooded boys like us. But we liked the music and the minister's prayer, which wasn't too long, and his sermon which was easy to understand and wasn't too long either. Then they had what they call testimonies, and different people stood up and said nice things about Jesus and how they loved Him and how their prayers were answered—things like that. I just sat there kinda trembly on the inside 'cause I loved Jesus too, maybe as much as any of them did. And I was wishing the minister would say, "Now if any of the boys and girls would like to say a word, we'll ask all the older people to keep still for a few minutes," but he didn't. So I just sat there wishing I'd get up anyway, and didn't, half promising myself I'd do it next Thursday night even if they didn't ask for boys and girls to. Hadn't Jesus died for boys and girls as well as for grown-ups? Even if I didn't know very much about it, I knew I loved Him anyway.

Poetry didn't get up either, he being bashful on account of his voice being squawky, although I reckon that wouldn't really have made any difference to the Lord if Poetry really loved Him.

Well, pretty soon, while the minister was talking again, Poetry and I almost jumped out of our seats when he said, "This afternoon I was called to the hospital to see a man who is supposed to be a bank robber. He was just a young man too. Poor boy! He was all broken up about it, said he hadn't done anything

45

wrong and was out there in the swamp looking for something."

Poetry's hand was gripping my arm so tight I could hardly keep from saying, "Ouch."

Then our minister asked us to pray for him that he might be saved because he wasn't sure the boy'd ever get well and even if he did get well, he ought to be saved anyway.

Maybe Poetry and I didn't pray out loud like some of the rest of them did, including my dad, but we prayed quietly anyway, even if our eyes were wide open. Say, there wasn't anybody in the world that could pray better than my dad could, not even a minister. Pop prayed especially for that boy in the hospital, and then for all the boys in our neighborhood and for all the boys in the world who, he said, would all grow up to be either good or bad men according to whether they became Christians when they were boys.

I guess Poetry must have felt like I did 'cause I saw him put his hand up to his eye real quick-like and brush away something. I was thinking what if that boy had been one of the Sugar Creek Gang, or even Poetry or me. Of course, he was eighteen years old, and I was only ten and Poetry about eleven or maybe almost twelve.

Well, the next morning my dad drove away in our car and was gone for about an hour and a half. When he came home he said he'd been to the hospital to see Barry Boyland, which was the name of the robber, if he was one.

"He's better," Dad said, "and the doctor thinks he'll get well in maybe a week or two." Dad was kinda happy too. I saw him take his big black Bible out of the car and carry it into the house and lay it on the center table.

"What else?" Mom said.

"Even if he doesn't get well, it'll be all right," Dad told her, "because he took Christ into his heart this morning, and he's saved now."

Mom seemed awful glad to hear that 'cause she liked boys so well and wanted them all to be saved. "And he wasn't a bank robber at all?" she asked.

"They don't know yet. He says he wasn't. Says he lived out in California, that his parents were dead, that he used to have an uncle that lived around here somewhere, and he had come to look him up. I asked him why he had been carrying a gun and he said somebody told him there were bears up in the hills and he was afraid not to, and that when he saw the sheriff and his posse he was so scared his gun accidentally discharged. They thought he was shooting at them, and because he had black hair like the robber was supposed to have had, they shot back at him.

"Just to prove he was really telling the truth," Dad went on, "he showed me a picture of his uncle which he had with him, and I've brought it home for you to see."

47

Dad took out of his pocket a picture which was about the size of a postcard. Mom gasped like she was terribly surprised and said, *"Old Man Paddler! Why—why!"*

"Let me see!" I said, getting there as quickly as I could.

"It's nothing," Dad said, not wanting to get me excited. "It's just the picture of an old man who used to live up in the hills but who disappeared about ten years ago when you were a little baby."

Dad handed the picture to me and it was my turn to be surprised. In fact, I never was so surprised in my life before 'cause the picture looked exactly like Poetry did when he had on the wig and long whiskers.

"What's the matter?" Dad asked.

"Nothing," I said, then added, "did he really die ten years ago?"

"He must have," Dad said, "although nobody seems to know what became of him. His old cabin is still up in the hills where it was, and people say it's haunted, maybe because nobody knows what happened to the old man. Anyway, I told Barry Boyland his uncle was dead, and he seemed very much disappointed."

Well, you can guess that I, Bill Collins, was listening for all I was worth to what Dad was saying, and thinking and thinking and trying to figure things out. The way Dad described the robber, he was the same one we'd seen yesterday digging around in the old hollow tree. I kept thinking about the wig and the whiskers and the dark glasses which Poetry'd found and the funny map with the old man in bed. I thought maybe Barry's uncle must have been a crazy old hermit or something. Maybe he even drew the map himself, and maybe he buried it there in the old tree, and buried the disguise there too. *But why?* I asked myself.

Well anyway, maybe we boys'd find out this afternoon. Now that we knew there wasn't anything particular to be afraid of, it would be like some new game, only a whole lot more mysterious.

Pretty soon it was dinner time. Right after that it was one o'clock and the gang was all down at the spring: Circus, Dragonfly, Poetry, Little Jim with his gunnysack, Big Jim with his tape measure, and me, Bill Collins.

First I told them what Dad had said about the robber not being a robber at all and about him being saved. You should have heard Little Jim sigh with relief just like he'd been carrying something heavy for a long time and somebody had suddenly lifted it off his shoulders. Even Circus seemed glad. There happened to be an elm sapling right there, and he shinned up it as quick as a squirrel and stood up on the first limb, slapped his hands against his legs like an old rooster flapping his wings after he's just won a fight with another rooster, and then Circus crowed in a way that sounded exactly like our old red rooster at home.

Well, we called a meeting and decided we'd start

looking for the treasure, or whatever it was, right away 'cause maybe if we found it we could help pay the hospital bill of Barry Boyland. You see if he didn't have any parents, maybe he wouldn't have enough money to pay it himself. And if he *was* a robber, well, then maybe we'd find the stolen money and get a reward. So pretty soon we were all there at the old tree again measuring off twenty yards, which is the same as sixty feet, you know.

Well, it looked like sixty feet was going to be right under the biggest rosebush of all, with the sharpest thorns. We measured all over again to be sure, and as near as we could figure straight east, that was just where it was. And that meant that whatever was buried there, if anything, must have been buried before the rosebush started to grow a long time ago. Well, we just walked round and round, all of us being barefoot. We couldn't decide what to do, when pretty soon Little Jim laid his gunnysack down right under the bush, laid himself down right on top of it, and started raking away the leaves and dead grass with his stick. Before we knew it, he'd found something 'cause we could hear his stick scraping on something hard. Big Jim got excited then and in a jiffy he was there too, digging away with his woodman's hatchet which he'd brought along. But we were all pretty disappointed at what they found: nothing but a flat rock about a foot wide, all overgrown with moss and half buried in the earth. We all stood there looking at it and feeling spooky, for you could see as plain as day that it wasn't any ordinary rock. The fact is, it looked a little bit like an old fashioned tombstone, like the kind we have in our church graveyard, only it was lying down, instead of standing up.

Big Jim was digging around it and was just about ready to pry it out and turn it over to see what was under it or else what was written on the other side when Dragonfly said, "Psst! Somebody's watching us! I saw him right over there in the bushes!"

I tell you it didn't take Big Jim long to cover that stone over with dead leaves and dried grass, nor for all of us to start acting natural. Poetry was the first one to get started, having maybe a hundred poems tucked away in his mind somewhere. He dropped flat on the ground—anyway as flat as he could—and made a mournful face and with his hand up to his head said:

"Humpty Dumpty sat on a wall,
Humpty Dumpty had a great fall;
All the king's horses and all the king's men
Couldn't put Humpty Dumpty together again."

Circus was already lying on his back, swinging his feet up and down, and saying, "One, two; one, two; one, two; up, down; up, down; whoa!" Big Jim crawled out from under the rosebush, rubbed his eyes, and scolded us for waking him up. He said it so loud and looked so fierce that for a minute we thought he meant it. Then he yawned and acted awful sleepy.

"Look, fellows!" I cried, holding up one of the roses I'd just picked, "Look at these pretty yellow stamens all around the green and white center! Why, this rose has only five petals!" I said surprised-like. A stamen, you know, is the organ in a flower that carries the pollen; and if flowers didn't have them, you could plant a million seeds and none of them would grow.

But none of the boys were paying any attention to me, so I started looking for birds with my binoculars, and in a jiffy I was looking at a big red-winged black-bird swinging in the top of a little tree along the creek, his scarlet shoulders shining in the sun.

I swung my binoculars around like I was looking for more birds, and in a jiffy I saw somebody, sure enough, right over in the bushes. And would you believe it! He looked like an old man with long white hair and whiskers, only he didn't have dark glasses on. Yes, sir, he looked exactly like the picture I had seen of Old Man Paddler less than two hours ago.

I lowered my binoculars quick and looked around to see if Poetry was still with us, and he was.

Well, that meant we'd have to stop looking for the treasure now and wait till we were sure nobody was watching us. In fact, Big Jim said we'd better all go in swimming and come back later. We were just starting to leave when the man came out from where he was hiding and began hobbling toward us looking like an awful old man. You could tell he was angry about something for he waved his stick at us and shouted, "Get out of here! Don't you know this property belongs to me, you little rascals! Get out, I say, run! Or I'll have the law on you!"

"It's Old Man Paddler!" I cried and started to run. In a jiffy the whole gang was running helter-skelter through the woods just as fast as we could go, and we didn't stop until we got to the spring where we all dropped down on the grass and rested a minute so as to catch our breath and get cooled off before drinking. That's what you're supposed to do when you're hot, no matter how thirsty you are.

"Did you ever see a man so mad in your life?" Dragonfly asked.

"I never did," Circus said, filling one of the paper cups and drinking.

Of course, we'd all heard about Old Man Paddler living up in the hills a long time ago. We'd been up to his cabin two or three times. But he was supposed to be dead now. Everybody said so. But we'd seen him with our own eyes this afternoon, hadn't we? How can a man be dead and still be alive?

"Maybe we saw his ghost," Circus said. "My dad says this old swamp is haunted, but I never believed it before."

"There aren't any such things as ghosts," Little Jim said quickly, " 'cause my mother says the Bible says that when a man's dead, he's dead for good, and that

53

if he doesn't go to heaven, then he goes to that—that other place, and nobody ever comes back again."

Somehow we all knew Little Jim was right, he being a real Christian. But I decided to ask Dad about it when I got home that night.

Anyway Big Jim still had the map. He said it probably belonged to the old man and we'd have to give it back to him. Maybe he had something buried there himself, and after being away for ten years or more, he'd come back to get it.

We decided not to go back today but to keep it a secret about the old man 'cause we didn't want our folks to worry about us.

When I got home I had the grandest surprise waiting for me and you'd never guess it in the world. "Let's hurry and get your chores done, Bill," Dad said. "You've been such a good boy that you may stay all night at Thompsons, and you and Poetry can sleep out in their backyard in his tent."

Well, that was something I'd been wanting to do ever since school was out and Poetry had put up his tent. You can guess I didn't waste much time helping Dad with the chores, even if ordinarily I am kinda lazy about it.

9

SLEEPING in that big canvas tent with Poetry was the most fun I'd had in a long time. It was what is called a "wall tent," about eight feet high in the center and four feet high at the side walls with about eight inches of sod cloth all around the bottom, and with a drop screen in front to keep out mosquitoes. Only there weren't many mosquitoes around in our neighborhood because we boys, and my dad especially, poured oil on the surface of all the ponds and puddles in the swamp, being careful not to leave any water standing around in tin cans or kettles or things 'cause that's where mosquitoes breed.

You know, mosquitoes are funny things. The kind we have in our neighborhood are what Dad calls the "Culex" kind, which don't carry any disease such as malaria or yellow fever. Dad knows the scientific names for the kinds that do carry diseases, but they're too hard for me to pronounce and I can't spell them anyway.

As I said, mosquitoes are crazy things—crazy looking and crazy acting. Did you ever see those little wrigglers swimming around in your folks' rain barrel or in a can of water or something? Well, those ugly little "wiggle tails" as Little Jim calls them, are baby mosquitoes that have hatched out of eggs which their mother laid in the water. Well, those little wrigglers keep growing and growing and wriggling until they're as big as they'll ever get. And then all of a sudden they stop wriggling and float up to the surface of the water. They lie there just like they are dead until pretty soon the skin bursts open all the way along the back and out crawls a full grown mosquito. She flies away all ready to stick her sharp nose into somebody, inject a little poison, and suck out some blood—if she doesn't get slapped good and hard first. Say, does a mosquito bite ever itch! But if you put some soda water on it real quick, it'll feel a lot better right away.

Well, my dad drove me over to Poetry's house and let me out at the front gate. "Be sure to be a good boy," he said, which I didn't like to hear very well because I'd heard it maybe a million times in my life already—a thousand times anyway. I guess maybe I needed it though. Anyway I wouldn't have liked it if my dad had wanted me to be bad, would you? So I called out cheerfully, "I will!" I was willing to promise most anything because Dad had been so good to let me stay all night with Poetry in his tent.

I carried my little brown suitcase proudly up the walk and around the house to where Poetry's tent was pitched under a big maple tree. Poetry was so glad to see me you would have thought he hadn't seen me for a whole year. He lifted up the drop screen at the front of the tent, which was made of what is called "bobbinet" with a wide band of cheese cloth all around it for a border so it wouldn't tear so easy or wear out so quick.

Pretty soon we were inside, and say, it was grand! There were two cots, one on each side with an aisle about three feet wide between them. In a corner, Poetry had a nice little table with books and things on it, things such as a pocketknife, a compass, and Poetry's little black leather New Testament. Poetry was the kind of Christian that was brave and wasn't ashamed to let anybody know about it, while at the same time he was an honest-to-goodness boy that everybody liked. Maybe he was a little more mischievous than some boys, but I felt proud to have a friend like him for my very best friend.

Pretty soon it would be dark in the tent, so we decided to go outside. "I'm glad you brought your binoculars," Poetry said, " 'cause we might need them before morning." He didn't explain what he meant. However, we used them right away, looking around at different things. By standing up on Poetry's chicken house, we could look away across the field and see the chimney of our house and the big green ivy vine that almost covered the whole south side. You could see the big south window of my upstairs room which I always kept open when I slept, even in winter. That was one of the reasons why I had such good health.

Pretty soon, while Poetry and I were standing up on their chicken house talking and thinking and liking each other awful well, Poetry's dad called out sharply from the barn, "Leslie Thompson! Get down off there right this minute! You're too heavy for that roof! Don't you know it might smash in and kill a half dozen of your mother's finest laying hens?"— not mentioning the fact that it might smash Poetry too.

"All right," Poetry called and started to obey. "I only weigh a hundred and forty pounds," he said to me. "I guess my being so short makes me look like two hundred."

In a little while it was dark, so we told Poetry's folks good night and went inside the tent where Poetry struck a match which he took out of a waterproof match box, the kind everybody ought to have when they go camping. In a jiffy there was plenty of light to see to undress by coming from a little kerosene lamp on the table in the corner.

We'd already washed our feet good in an old foot tub just outside the tent door and had put on our slippers, Poetry's Mom making sure we did it so we wouldn't get her nice clean sheets all dirty.

I guess nothing feels better than sleeping in a tent when you're a boy. We felt like real campers or forest rangers or something. Pretty soon we had on our pajamas and were sitting on the edges of our cots kinda hating to turn out the light and crawl in. And I was wondering which one of us was going to say his prayers first. Maybe Poetry was thinking the same thing 'cause pretty soon he reached over, got his New

Testament, handed it to me, and said, "Let's read our chapters together tonight." I guess I forgot to tell you that Poetry and I had promised each other we'd read a chapter out of the New Testament at least once each day and that we'd pray for each other by name every night.

Well, I turned to the book of Acts, which is the fifth book of the New Testament, and read about fifteen verses. Anyway it was the story about Paul and Silas having to go to jail for preaching the gospel and how they sang songs at midnight and were so happy 'cause they loved Jesus so much in spite of being in jail with their feet all fastened tight in big wooden clamps or something. Then there was a big earthquake, and the jailer tried to kill himself with a sword. But instead he became a Christian, and he and his whole family were baptized before morning. It was a great story, I tell you, and we liked it a lot, Poetry and I kinda liking each other like Paul and Silas did. We made up our minds that if ever we had to go to jail for being Christians we'd do it, and we'd sing at midnight too, only we wouldn't exactly want any earthquake.

Then the two of us got down on our knees together beside Poetry's bed and said our prayers, only this time Poetry didn't say his little poem prayer at all but just talked to the heavenly Father with his own words. He explained afterward that he was getting a little bit too big to just quote a little poem to God, so he'd decided to talk to Him right out, knowing that He loved boys and that Jesus had been a boy once Himself.

Soon the lights were out and we were lying there in our cots, thinking and talking and telling each other stories and looking through the little square hole at the top of the tent entrance which was open for fresh air. We looked up at the sky with the stars looking down at us like they were our best friends, when Poetry started to say:

> "Twinkle, twinkle, Little Star,
>   How I wonder what you are!
> Up above the world so high,
>   Like a diamond in the sky."

I always did like that poem, ever since I was little, so I made him quote all of it, liking especially the verse which goes:

> "In the dark blue sky you keep,
>   And often through my curtains peep;
> For you never shut your eye,
>   Till the sun is in the sky."

Then we began to get sleepy and in a minute we were gone. Say, did you ever wonder where a boy goes when he goes to sleep? Of course you don't really go anywhere 'cause when you wake up, why you're still right there in bed. Well, anyway, I was when I awakened a little later by the queerest noise coming from up in the old maple tree somewhere right above our heads. It sounded like somebody was crying or else moaning or wailing in a trembly voice. Of course as soon as I was awake I knew it was nothing but a screech owl and nothing to be afraid of. I'd seen plenty of them in the daytime. They generally sit all alone in a hole in some old tree, sound asleep, waiting for night to come so they can go mouse hunting or maybe cutworm hunting. Dad says they're one of the farmer's best friends because at night cutworms cause the most trouble, cutting off the little corn shoots and beans and things like that. Since the screech owls hunt them at night, killing hundreds of them, boys ought never to kill any screech owls no matter how much they don't like them.

Poetry was awake too, and pretty soon he whispered, "Bill!"

"What!" I whispered back.

"I've got an idea."

I was still pretty sleepy so I just grunted.

"Remember Old Man Paddler?" Poetry asked.

That woke me up quicker'n anything. "Yes," I said, and then that screech owl let out another long, trembly wail that sent the shivers up and down my spine. It's a whole lot different when you're home and upstairs in bed listening to an owl out in the woods than it is sleeping in a tent, which is about the same as sleeping out of doors.

But Poetry didn't pay any attention. He said, "I

asked my dad a lot of questions about Old Man Paddler when I got home tonight without telling him anything, and he said that he was the kindest old man that ever lived and that he especially liked boys!"

I didn't answer, just waiting to see what else Poetry'd have to say 'cause I knew he'd thought of something important. I could hear his bed springs squeaking like he was getting up. "Wait'll I scare that owl away and I'll tell you," he said.

He fumbled around for his flashlight, turned it on a minute, stepped into his slippers, raised the tent flap, and went out with me following right behind him, both of us in our pajamas, looking like a couple of ghosts. He turned the flashlight up into the tree and for a minute we saw Mr. Owl with his cat-like eyes blinking and looking very fierce and disgusted at us for not appreciating his entertainment. Then he spread his wings and flew like a shadow across the garden toward the barn.

Maybe I forgot to tell you that that old sycamore tree down along the swamp was nearer to Poetry's house than it was to any of the rest of the gang's, being maybe not more than a quarter of a mile away. To get to it from Poetry's house you had to go down a hill and through the woods. Well, we were standing there in the moonlight after the owl had flown away, when Poetry said so sudden-like that it startled me, "If Old Man Paddler liked boys and was kind to them, and was even a Christian, as Dad says he was, then that wasn't him we saw today! Do you know what I think? I think the man we saw today was wearing a wig and false whiskers. I saw his hands and they weren't any more an old man's hands than anything. I'll bet he's some robber or somebody that's trying to make people think he's Old Man Paddler so he can fool Barry Boyland and get the treasure. And I'll bet Barry knows there's a map and that when his uncle died he left his money somewhere and he's coming back to get it."

"But what about the disguise you found in the tree?" I asked. I couldn't figure out what Poetry was driving at.

"They belonged to the man we saw today. When I found them, he had to get some new ones."

Well, that sounded sensible, and I told Poetry so.

"Also," Poetry said, just like a real detective explaining things, "as long as Barry Boyland is in the hospital, it's up to us boys to protect his interests."

"Maybe we ought to tell the police," I said, thinking what my dad would say we ought to do.

"Not on your life! Think we want to have them spoil our fun?"

Well, I didn't want to argue with Poetry. Besides, his ideas were nearly always right.

We started to go back into the tent when he stopped so quick I bumped into him. "Listen!" he said.

I didn't hear anything but I did see something that

looked like a light down in the woods, maybe not far from the sycamore tree.

"Get your binoculars quick!" Poetry commanded under his breath. He handed me his flashlight, and in a jiffy I was in the tent and out again and Poetry was looking through my binoculars down the hill toward where we knew the tree was.

"Look!" he whispered and handed the binoculars to me. All I could see was a light and a shadow moving about it.

"We've got to do something quick!" Poetry said. "We won't even have time to dress." In a jiffy he was in the tent and out again with the disguise he'd found in the old tree day before yesterday.

"What are you going to do?" I asked, my teeth chattering—and not because I was cold either, for it was a warm night. I noticed particularly that Poetry had on his big shoes, so I put mine on too, real quick.

"Let's go or we'll be too late!" he said. Well, I didn't exactly want to run smack into any ghosts or whatever was down along the swamp but I didn't want to seem like a coward either. So I followed him as fast as I could. The wind was blowing on our faces so we knew whoever was there wouldn't hear us coming unless we made a lot of noise.

Say, Poetry looked ridiculous in his big, flapping white pajamas, and I guess I looked just as ridiculous running after him. He knew every inch of the woods along the creek here, so we just hurried along, me thinking his idea was still crazy—well, *dangerous* anyway.

When we got to the bottom of the hill we stopped to get our breath and to look through the binoculars again. As plain as day we could see an old-fashioned lantern and a man was digging with a spade right beside the swamp rosebush where we'd been digging that afternoon.

"We'll have to hurry!" Poetry said excitedly. "Look what a big hole he's got already!"

We stooped down low and crawled along as quiet as we could until we were real close, so close if we'd made any noise he'd have heard us and that would have spoiled everything. And we could see the man too, the same old man we'd seen in the afternoon, with the long white hair and the long beard, and he was working terribly fast.

Then I looked at Poetry and guessed what he was going to do, for he was putting on the whiskers and the wig which he had brought with him. "Listen," he whispered in my ear, "you lie flat on the ground right here, and when I let out a long ghost laugh, you turn the flashlight on me quick, and leave it on until I start moaning and talking crazy, and then you turn it off. When I start laughing again, you turn it on again quick!"

Poetry stood up then and started waving his arms like a crazy man, and then with that squawky voice of his that sounded more like a ghost than any real ghost

65

could have sounded, he let out a blood-curdling wail that sounded like a screech owl with a bad cold. I turned the flashlight on him just as he started that wailing. Honest, if I didn't know who it was, I'd have been scared almost to death, for he was waving his arms, and his pajamas were flapping crazily, and it was enough to scare anybody.

Then Poetry started the awfullest moaning you ever heard and saying slowly, *"I . . . am . . . Old . . . Man . . . Paddler's . . . GHOST!"* yelling the word *ghost* real loud but with a low voice like a man's voice. Then Poetry let out that terrible laugh and sent the shivers up and down my spine again, and I turned the flashlight on him and watched him waving his white pajamas and looking even worse than a ghost.

Well, sir, that man dropped his spade and looked around like he was awful scared. In a flash he jumped up and dashed lickety-sizzle straight toward Poetry with both hands stretched out in front of him like he was going to grab Poetry and choke him to death.

But just that second two shadows darted out from behind some bushes. One of them made a dive for the man's legs in real football style, and a voice— it was Big Jim's voice—yelled for us to come and help. I tell you I was glad to hear Big Jim's voice. To tell the truth I was pretty badly scared, not wanting to let Poetry know it. It turned out that Big Jim and Circus, who lived right across the road from each other, had decided maybe they'd better stand on guard tonight for fear somebody would spoil everything, and so they'd hidden themselves in the bushes, having gotten there just a few minutes before we did, coming up the creek from the other direction.

In a jiffy all four of us boys, Big Jim, Circus, Poetry, and I were scrambling all over that man. His old white hair and whiskers came off just like Poetry thought they would and we saw he had black hair, the same color as the radio had said the bank robber was supposed to have had. Say, he struck out with his big fists and kicked and swore. One of his fists caught me on the chin and knocked me flat, but it didn't hurt much 'cause I was so mad, and things don't seem to hurt so much when you are. Anyway, you don't feel them at the time. But I didn't stay down. In a second I was right in there in the thick of the fight. I got there just in time to see Poetry's big right foot with his heavy shoe on it kick the man right on the shin of his right leg, and I heard the man let out a yell of pain. I was glad right that minute that Poetry had big feet.

I dived in head first and got hold of one of the man's legs, and Circus grabbed the other. We held on like a couple of bull dogs, or maybe like a couple of snapping turtles holding onto a boy's toe. Pretty soon we had the man down on his stomach, with Poetry lying right across this shoulders and head. Big Jim knew all the best wrestling tricks, and as I told you before, he was terribly strong. Well, he'd gotten that man's arm behind him in what is called the "arm grape vine hold" and that's how it had been so easy for us to get him down and keep him there, in spite of the man's yelling and kicking and swearing and threatening to kill us.

Afterward we learned another reason why it had been so easy to keep him down, for when he was locked up in jail next day, he had one eye swollen almost shut where Big Jim had hit him with his fist in the fight we'd had. It took Big Jim's knuckles almost a week to get completely well, he'd hit the man so hard.

Anyway, that's where Little Jim's gunnysack came in handy, for we'd left it there, you know, when we'd been scared away in the afternoon. As I told you, Big Jim knew how to tie twenty-one different kinds of knots. Well, he knew how to make ropes too. He took his knife and cut that sack into strips and twisted them together. In almost no time we had that robber's legs and hands tied so he couldn't get away.

After we got him tied, we didn't know what to do with him. "What'll we do with him?" Big Jim asked.

"Let's bury him," Circus suggested, not meaning it, of course. "He's got his grave already dug."

Say, that started our prisoner to swearing like I'd never heard any man swear in my life. I was glad Little Jim wasn't there 'cause he just naturally loved Jesus so much that when anybody used His name like that it made Little Jim feel terribly bad.

The man began to kick and squirm and try to get loose, not knowing that Big Jim was an expert at tying knots. Then all of a sudden Circus let out a yell and picked up something shiny that had been lying right there on the ground by the man's lantern. At first I could hardly believe my eyes, but there it was in Circus' hand as plain as day—a real honest to goodness revolver! I guess our faces were pretty sober right then for we realized how serious things were, and how maybe one of us might have been shot or killed. I didn't tell any of the boys, although I did tell Poetry later, but I just shut my eyes for a minute and whispered a thank you prayer. "Dear God," I said, "thank you for not letting any of us boys get killed." And I *was* thankful too, I can tell you.

Big Jim took the gun, opened it, and saw that it was loaded. Then he said grimly in a voice that sounded awful fierce, "And now, Mr. Whoever-you-are, I've got your gun pointing right straight toward you! You lie still while we get the sheriff!"

Poetry was delegated to run home for his dad, which he did. His dad phoned the sheriff and then came down himself to help us guard the robber until the sheriff got there. After that we all went home and went to bed.

69

10

OF COURSE we didn't get to sleep right away because we were pretty excited and so tickled we didn't know what to do. I guess that man must have thought Poetry was a real ghost or else Old Man Paddler come to life again, or he wouldn't have been so scared. Anyway that's what I thought that night while we were going back to Poetry's tent. We'd gotten to the rosebush just in time, too, for right down in the hole where the robber had been digging we'd found a rusty steel box which must have been buried by Old Man Paddler himself.

Of course, as Poetry's dad said while we were all waiting there in the lantern light for the sheriff to come, taking turns holding that steel box on our laps, "Barry Boyland will have to prove he is really and truly the old man's nephew before his treasure, or whatever it is, will be given to him."

Well, at last Poetry and I were on our cots again with the same stars looking down at us through the opening in the tent, and with the same wind sighing through the leaves in the maple overhead. We got sleepier and sleepier, and the next thing we knew, it was morning.

Maybe I never told you that if it hadn't been for the gang, I'd have been real lonesome. You see, I didn't have any brothers or sisters. When you're the only child in the house, you keep wishing and wishing you weren't. I guess I wanted a little brother as much as I wanted anything in the world.

Anyway, when I told Poetry good-bye that morning, I couldn't help but think how nice it would be to have just one brother, even if he was littler than me.

I was still feeling that way about it when I came up to the back door of our house carrying my suitcase. Just then Dad came hurrying toward the house from the barn with his teeth shining under his moustache and with the happiest smile on his face you ever saw. First he picked me up in his big strong arms and whirled me around in a circle, crying "Hurrah! Hurrah! Bill Collins!" as if he was tickled to death to see me. I thought maybe he'd heard about us catching the robber and I could hardly wait until we got in the house so I could tell him and Mom. Then all of a sudden I heard a baby crying, and something inside of me just kinda bubbled up like it does when I want to tell Jesus I love Him, and I knew that a new baby had come to live with us.

"The grandest surprise for you!" Dad said. "The grandest brand new baby in the world!" And I could see myself having a little brother to play with and not being so lonesome any more when I was at home.

"A brother?" I asked, hoping it wasn't a girl. In fact, I'd made up my mind to be mad if it was 'cause I wanted a little brother so bad.

71

"It's a girl!" Dad said, "The prettiest, blue-eyed, curly-haired little sister a boy ever had given to him!" Dad was so tickled he couldn't keep still. He picked up my suitcase and said, "Come on, Bill Collins, and see our little Charlotte Ann!"

Now why in the world I didn't like the name Charlotte Ann I didn't know, but I didn't want a baby sister either. So I hung back, not wanting to get into the house. I was disappointed too 'cause I wanted them to be all excited over our catching the robber, supposing of course they'd heard about it. But instead they were making a big fuss over the new baby.

I went into the kitchen, but not a step farther.

"Well, Bill Collins!" Dad said, surprised. "Aren't you glad?"

The fact is, I wasn't. I didn't like girls very well, I'll have to admit.

But I guess Dad understands boys, for he didn't make me go in. He just went in himself, and pretty soon I could hear him and Mom talking about me, and also making funny cooing noises to the baby. "He wanted a little brother," Dad said. Mom answered something I couldn't hear, and then I heard some other woman talking too. Just to be sure I wasn't missing anything I peeped around the corner of the door and saw that the other woman had on a nurse's uniform. I decided to go outdoors, which I did.

Dad had planted some early potatoes in a special garden down along the orchard next to the road, and they were already up and growing. So I went to the toolhouse and got the hoe and started hoeing those potatoes without being told to.

I stayed mad all morning and wouldn't go into the house at all. Dad just let me work and work without saying much of anything to me. He was plowing in the field behind our orchard, and I noticed he was whistling and singing all morning. Every half hour, or even less, he'd tie the horses up at the fence and go to the house to see the new baby. It looked like I wasn't going to be so important around our home any more.

About eleven o'clock I began to feel worse and worse. Two or three times I got mad at myself even because tears came into my eyes. I felt so sorry for myself. But I began to get awful hungry, and I decided maybe I'd just go in at noon and eat dinner anyway. That is, if they'd have a plate set for me.

Well, just when I was feeling the worst, Dragonfly came along, stopped on the other side of the fence, and said, "Hello, Bill!"

"Hello," I said without looking up. My hoe slipped and I cut off one of the biggest potatoes in the garden. But I didn't care. I just took my hoe and chopped the potato to pieces and covered it up and went on hoeing, after wiping the sweat off my forehead with my hand.

"What's the matter?" Dragonfly asked. "What are you so mad about?"

73

"Nothing," I said, "except I've got a new baby sister!" I kept on hoeing.

Dragonfly looked kinda glum and didn't say a word for a minute. Then he asked, "How old is she?"

"I don't know," I said.

"I'll bet she's ugly," he said. "Girls always are when they're little."

Say, do you know I didn't like to hear Dragonfly say that? In fact, I resented it. "She's pretty," I said, forgetting that I hadn't even looked at her. "She's got pretty blue eyes and black curls!"

"Yeah, but she's a girl, though."

I sighed, still disgusted, and said, "Yeah, that's the trouble."

"But as soon as she is big enough, you won't have to help with the dishes any more," he said.

That was the first encouraging thing I'd thought of all morning, so I kinda sighed. Since there was a peach tree right close by with a lot of nice shade under it, Dragonfly and I lay down in the grass and talked a long time about different things, mostly about last night and Old Man Paddler. Say, Dragonfly was surprised, and he felt pretty bad to think he hadn't been there to help us catch the robber. We kept on talking until Dad called me to dinner. Then Dragonfly got up and hurried home, suddenly remembering his mom had told him not to come over to my house this morning.

It seemed funny for Dad to call me to dinner when all my life I'd been used to having Mom do it, but then I supposed she had to take care of the new baby.

At the table Dad prayed a little longer than usual. He was so happy on account of me having a little sister. Mom wasn't feeling very well, so she didn't come to the table at all. Besides, she had to take care of the baby. The nurse carried a tray in to Mom and then came back and sat in her place at the table. It didn't seem right to have another woman sitting there, and I got to thinking maybe right after dinner I'd better go in the other room and see Mom anyway. If the baby was there, I'd just sorta look at it kinda quick without particularly noticing it.

Well, pretty soon dinner was over and I went over to the corner of the dining room where I always kept my straw hat. Neither Dad nor the nurse paid any attention to me, anyway not so I could notice it. I kept looking at the door to the other room out of the corner of my eye, wanting to go in and pretending to be having trouble with one of the buckles on my overall suspender. Then without hardly knowing I was going to, I sidled into the room. And there was Mom in bed with the happiest smile on her face you ever saw. Beside her, snuggled real close and kinda lying in the crook of Mom's arm, was the baby.

I guess I never did feel so bashful in my life. I stood there holding my straw hat in both hands looking down at my bare feet.

"Come here a minute," Mom said. I walked over close to the bed and started looking at some roses in a vase on a table. I guess those were the prettiest roses in the world. They were about the color of the goldenrod writing paper we used in school, only the petals were soft like velvet. Dad had sent clear to Australia to get the seed and he'd grown them himself out in our garden. Say, those yellow roses had the sweetest perfume! Their color made me think of a whole bed of wild fawn lilies which I'd seen down along the creek only yesterday. I guess the real name for fawn lilies is "dogtooth violet," only Dad says they aren't violets. There *were* some blue and purple violets right close by that bed of fawn lilies, though.

So pretty soon I said to Mom, "Do you think she'd like a bouquet of flowers from down along the creek? Maybe I'll have time to go pick some for her."

"I'm sure she would," Mom said, and her face was happier than ever. Honest, I'd never seen Mom so happy in my life, and I could tell by the way she looked at me that she didn't like my little sister a bit better'n she did me.

In about a minute I was out of doors climbing over the fence and running like a deer through the woods, following the little footpath to the spring. I was going to pick the biggest bouquet of flowers anybody ever saw for little Charlotte Ann.

Well, I was stooping down right in the middle of

that bed of fawn lilies when pretty soon I heard somebody coming. It was Circus.

"Hello, Bill!" he said, "What you doin'?"

"Nothing," I said. "I got a new baby sister." And
I went on picking flowers, suddenly remembering Circus didn't like girls very well.

"I thought you wanted a little brother!" Circus
grunted, as if he was disgusted with me for not getting
what I wanted.

"She's awful nice," I said, "black hair and blue
eyes and—"

"I've got three sisters," Circus said, "and they've all
got blue eyes. There ain't anything special about blue
eyes." Just then he saw a tree he'd never climbed before, and in a jiffy he was halfway up to the first limb.
It made me plumb disgusted the way he talked. *Whatever made him not like girls anyway?* I thought.

Pretty soon the whole gang was there except Big
Jim who had to do some work before he could come.

"Bill's got a baby sister!" Circus called down to the
gang from where he was sitting, looking like a chim-
panzee there on the first limb of the tree.

"Yeah, and she's got blue eyes and long black curls,"
Dragonfly said, teasing me.

"He's picking flowers for her," Poetry said. *Even
Poetry is teasing me,* I thought. They all knew how
I wanted a little brother.

I just kept on picking flowers, getting madder every
minute and liking my little sister better than ever.

"I'll help you," Little Jim said. "I'll bet she'll like these," starting to pick some harebells over by a beech tree on the bark of which all of us boys had carved our initials. It was the kind of tree you could do that on.

Little Jim always did stick up for a fellow when he was getting teased. In a minute Poetry acted like he was ashamed for having said anything, so he lay down in the grass and started picking flowers himself and saying,

> "Butter cups and daisies,
> Oh the pretty flowers;
> Coming ere the springtime,
> To tell of sunny hours;
> While the trees are leafless,
> While the fields are bare . . ."

Only the trees weren't leafless and the fields weren't bare.

Well, I finished my bouquet and ran home with them as fast as I could. Little Jim went with me 'cause he wanted to see the baby too.

"What's her name?" he asked, panting for breath.

"Charlotte Ann."

"It's a pretty name," he said. "I wish I had a little sister." And right then I decided I liked Little Jim an awful lot, almost as well as Poetry.

When we got back to the gang, Big Jim was there. We all lay around in the grass talking about what had happened last night and explaining to Dragonfly and Little Jim that we couldn't help it 'cause they weren't there to get in on the fun. We all kept looking at Big Jim's sore knuckle and kinda envying him for being able to hit the robber so hard it almost knocked him unconscious.

Then we all decided to go up to look at the sycamore tree and the big hole in the ground, and then, Big Jim said, we'd go up into the hills to see the cabin where Old Man Paddler used to live.

Pretty soon we were all standing around the hole by the big swamp rosebush and being glad the robber was safe in jail where he couldn't hurt anybody. We could see the grass all mashed down where we'd had our fight.

Little Jim just walked around with a sober face, thinking when all of a sudden he said, "I'll bet if I'd been here and had got a hold of one of his legs, I wouldn't have let go!"

"He only had *two* legs," Dragonfly said, "and Bill and Circus had both of them."

Little Jim looked disappointed for a minute, then his face kinda lit up and he said, "But I could have helped *sit* on him after you got him down, couldn't I?"

Of course he could, I thought, but Dragonfly spoiled it by saying, "Not with Poetry sitting on him too. There wouldn't have been room enough!"

We all lay down in the grass and Poetry and I told the whole story all over again, not forgetting to tell how ridiculous Poetry looked in his big flapping pajamas with the long hair and whiskers on. Then Big Jim called a meeting and gave us a little talk about crime never paying, and he quoted a kinda scary verse from the Bible which says: "Be not deceived; God is not mocked: for whatsoever a man soweth, that shall he also reap." Then he explained that if anybody lived a sinful life, he'd have to suffer for it some time not only in this life but in the life after this one. And he made us promise we'd never—any of us—ever steal anything as long as we lived.

When he got through, Little Jim piped up and said, "One of the Ten Commandments says 'Thou shalt not steal.' "

When the meeting was over and we were on our way up into the hills climbing toward Old Man Paddler's cabin, we felt as if we'd all been to church. I kept thinking as we walked along about that beautiful sunset I'd seen night before last with the sun shining through long colored clouds looking like a waterfall tumbling over a dam with colored electric lights behind it. And I remembered how pretty soon those clouds changed so they looked like the bars of a jail. One of the clouds especially had looked like an old man with long whiskers. I kept thinking about Old Man Paddler and wondering what he was doing up in heaven—if he was there and he was if he was dead 'cause Little Jim had said that if people let Jesus into their hearts while they were alive, He'd let them into heaven when they died. Of course my folks had taught me that too a long time ago, but Little Jim's saying it seemed to make it more true. He was such a good Christian.

Well, we had a lot of fun climbing up to that old cabin. We pretended that Big Jim was the sheriff and the rest of us were his posse and we were going up to ambush a band of robbers who lived there.

In about a half hour, I reckon, we were close enough to the cabin to see it. So we all stopped and lay down in the grass and made our plans as to how we'd capture those imaginary robbers. It made us feel kinda creepy to remember that some people believed the old house was haunted. Of course we knew that was because Old Man Paddler had just disappeared without anybody knowing what had become of him. Everybody finally decided he'd either drowned in the creek or else wandered too far off the path out into the dangerous part of the swamp and had sunk down into the quicksand.

Well, we made our plans and sneaked around from tree to tree and from bush to bush until we were real close to the cabin. All of a sudden Dragonfly said, "Psst!" We knew he'd either heard or seen something.

We all stopped dead in our tracks and listened, and I guess my red hair must have stood right up on end. I think we had all heard it at once—a sort of low moan like somebody was trying to call for help and couldn't 'cause his mouth was covered with a blanket or something.

11

I CLOSED MY TEETH together tight to keep them from chattering 'cause I didn't want anybody to know how scared I was. I noticed Big Jim look around quick to see if Little Jim was there and all right. It was grand the way he looked after that little fellow. He couldn't have liked him any better if they'd been brothers, I thought. And I made up my mind that even if Charlotte Ann wasn't a little boy, I was going to like her just as much as Big Jim liked Little Jim, and I'd protect her and take care of her too. Thinking that made me so I wasn't nearly as afraid as I was just a half a minute before.

We could see Big Jim was making up his mind to do something, for we could still hear that muffled voice in the cabin calling for help. I kept thinking what if whoever was in there was just trying to get us to come in to catch us in a trap! But we couldn't afford to lie there waiting if somebody was really needing us. So pretty soon Big Jim told us to keep still while he and Circus went to investigate.

In just about a minute we saw Circus standing in the doorway of the old cabin and motioning for us to come quick. I tell you, it didn't take us long to scramble to our feet and get there.

What do you think we saw the minute we got in? There were only two rooms in the cabin, and on a cot in the corner of one was an old man with long white hair and whiskers and with his hands and feet tied with strips of blanket. Big Jim was just taking a gag out of his mouth which somebody had put there to keep him from calling for help, I suppose. He looked exactly like the picture I'd seen of Old Man Paddler, the picture Barry Boyland had given my dad in the hospital yesterday morning. He also looked like the robber we'd caught last night before his wig and beard had come off.

"Water!" the old man cried in a broken voice. I thought of the map we'd found and of the picture of an old man in bed asking a nurse for more water. Dragonfly looked around quick and found an old tin can on a table. Then he and I ran out and down the hill to where we'd seen a spring on our way up.

"I wonder who he is," Dragonfly said, panting for breath.

"Old Man Paddler, of course," I said.

"But how can he be? He's dead!"

"He doesn't look like it, does he?"

"He's supposed to be anyway," Dragonfly said.

In about two minutes we were back with the water, and the old man drank it like he hadn't had any for a long time. We were careful not to let him drink too much or too fast 'cause it might not be good for him. Pretty soon he was sitting up in bed and thanking us boys for coming to his rescue. He'd been tied up here since yesterday, he said, and he hadn't had a drink since last night. Say, he had the kindest little gray eyes anybody ever saw, and you could tell by the way he looked at us that he liked boys. And that's how we decided he must be the real Old Man Paddler.

"You *aren't* a ghost, *are* you?" Little Jim asked. You could see he liked the old man an awful lot. Little Jim always did like old people and was kind to them.

That old man just laughed right out when Little Jim said that. He told us he'd left the hills about ten years ago and had traveled clear around the world visiting many countries.

Well, the old man said he had decided to come back home and live the rest of his life here in the hills—

Suddenly he stopped telling us about himself and looked around as if he were afraid. And that gave us an idea we ought to tell him about the robber being caught and his nephew getting shot and how his treasure was locked up in the big vault in the bank uptown right this minute—if it was really his treasure. So we told him, all of us helping a little bit.

You should have seen the worried look leave his face. All of a sudden he said, "I bet you boys are hungry." But we weren't. That is, we'd rather hear his side of the story first, how he happened to get tied up and anything he wanted to tell us.

"I'll bet *you're* hungry," Circus said. We began looking to see if there was anything to eat.

That robber we'd caught must have been living in Old Man Paddler's cabin for quite awhile, for he had laid in quite a supply of food—canned pork and beans and corn and all kinds of foods. Of course Old Man Paddler himself had brought some when he'd come home yesterday afternoon.

We carried in some wood and built a fire in the old stove and carried a kettle of water for him.

"I dug some sassafras roots yesterday just before coming home," he said, looking in a can on an old shelf. And sure enough he found some. "How'd you boys like to have some tea? It's very good for boys."

Sassafras tea, you know, is made from the sweet-smelling roots of the sassafras tree. The roots are kinda reddish color, and you cut them in little pieces and boil them in water till the water turns red. With sugar in it, it beats any other kind of tea all to pieces for taste. Anyway, I think so. Little Jim had never tasted any before, and he said it was just like drinking lollipop juice, that is, if there was such a thing

I don't suppose I can tell Old Man Paddler's story like he told it, and maybe it'll sound more like me telling it than him. But I'll do the best I can 'cause it's a real story. As I said, as soon as he heard about the robber being caught and put in jail, he didn't act worried or afraid anymore. So he had us sit down and listen. Big Jim sat on a chair with Little Jim on the cot beside him, and the rest of us sat or sprawled on the floor. The old man sat in the only other chair there was in the cabin, one he'd made years ago himself out of hickory mostly. Say, he looked just like one of the pictures of Moses I'd seen in my Bible story book at home, my parents having bought me one with a lot of pictures in it when I was little.

Old Man Paddler had been traveling around the world and visiting a lot of countries, staying maybe a month or two in each place. He was rich, you know. Then he got thinking maybe he was too old to travel any more, and if he died he ought to do something with all the money he'd buried back in the hills along the old swamp.

I guess if you'd seen us boys while he was telling us that story, with his kind old eyes looking at us as if we were his very own grandchildren, his long whiskers bobbing every time his chin moved, you'd have thought we all should have been named Dragonfly. That was the most exciting story we'd ever heard, and our eyes were almost popping out of our heads —well, anyway, they were wide open every minute of the story.

"When I got back from my trip around the world," Old Man Paddler said, "I was so tired I didn't feel very well. So I stopped down there by the old spring to get a drink and rest, wondering if anything had happened to my cabin while I was away. I hadn't intended to stay so long when I left, you know. Then

I looked up and saw smoke coming out of the chimney. *Who's in my cabin?* I thought. I hurried up the hill and pushed open the door. There sitting at my table and drinking coffee was a man that looked almost exactly like me. It was just like looking at my twin, or else in a mirror, and I began to wonder if maybe I was losing my mind or something, being so old.

" 'Who are you?' I asked. And the strange man just laughed and said, telling a lie, 'I'm Old Man Paddler, of course. What do you want?' And he swore at me.

"Well, right away I knew I hadn't lost my mind, and that the man wasn't *me,* because I didn't swear at all. Hadn't since I was a little boy and had let Jesus Christ come into my heart.

" 'You can't swear in my house!' I told him.

"Well, that man stood up and glared at me," Old Man Paddler said, "and then all of a sudden he grabbed me and pulled me inside and pointed a gun at me and shouted, 'I am Old Man Paddler! Do you hear? And you're just a visitor! Come here! I'm going to cut your whiskers off!'

"Well, I'm not very strong any more and I couldn't have done anything to protect myself, so all I could do was beg him not to. Anyway, he changed his mind and said he guessed he'd kill me and throw me into the swamp. 'Everybody thinks you're dead anyway and we'd just as well let it be true!' he said. First he tied me up and threw me on the bed. Then he got a mirror and came over to where I was and began looking into it. He'd look first at me, then into the mirror.

" 'I look exactly like you,' he said gruffly. 'I'm certainly glad you came home so I'll know exactly how I'm supposed to look.' He looked at himself in the mirror and laughed again.

"I had to admit he looked just like me. I kept lying there wishing my nephew would come. You see, about a week before I came home I'd sent a letter to my only living relative out in California telling him to please come to see me, as I was getting old and had a lot of money to give him before I died. In that letter I told him where he would find a map that would explain where I'd buried my money, so in case anything happened to me before he got here he'd know where to find it. I explained the map also, just in case he wouldn't be able to figure out what the different things meant."

The old man stopped a minute while we all sighed, waiting eagerly for him to finish. That map, you know, was the one we'd found in the old sycamore tree day before yesterday.

"Well," the old man went on with his story, while I shifted my feet to a more comfortable position, one of them having gone to sleep 'cause I was sitting on it, "my twin stood there glaring at me, trying to decide what he'd better do with me. I tell you boys, I'm an old man, and I thought maybe my time had come to die. So I just shut my eyes and started praying and

88

telling the Father in heaven I was ready if He wanted me. Then I remembered again all that money I'd buried and was going to give my nephew and maybe he wouldn't even get my letter and the money would be wasted. In my travels around the world, I'd seen so many places where missionaries were needed, and I thought that maybe in a few minutes I'd be in heaven seeing Jesus face to face and He'd ask me why I hadn't used some of that money for missionary work . . ."

Then the old man went on with his story—"Well, the robber heard me praying and it made him angry. 'Shut up!' he shouted, and raised his fist like he was going to hit me. So I did stop praying out loud, although I kept right on praying silently, knowing God could hear anyway, and telling Him I was ready to die because I knew He'd sent His Son, Jesus, to save me, and I had believed on Him in my heart.

" 'All right, Grandpa!' the fierce looking man said roughly, 'Let's get those whiskers off! Or shall I take you out somewhere and bury you?' He came over to me and took hold of my beard and gave it a little jerk. Then he laughed roughly and said, 'They're real whiskers all right, and your hair is genuine too. I lost a wig and beard just like the one I have on now down by the swamp a few days ago, and I may need another before I leave this country.' He stood there looking at me as if he were trying to think of some way to get mine off so he could use them himself in case he needed them.

"I could see he was a wicked man and might do anything. And with his gun pointing straight at me, I began to think how I might save my life for a little while at least, so I said, 'Maybe you'd like to know where my treasure is buried.' "

The old man stopped talking again and poured himself another cup of sassafras tea, then he went on with his story—"All the time I was hoping my nephew would come yet afraid to have him come because he might get hurt. So I told the robber where to dig, and he must have decided to let me live a little while longer, for he put a gag in my mouth and went away leaving me all tied up like you found me. Just as he went out the door, he said, 'Listen, Grandpa Paddler, if you've lied to me, I'll come back! And you can tell this world good-bye!' And that was the last I saw him."

The old man sighed like he was tired of talking. Anyway that was his side of the story, and you know what happened after that, how the robber had seen us boys digging there by the rosebush and that night had come back himself and we had captured him.

Well, we boys thanked him for telling us the story and promised to come back and see him again, and maybe we'd go see his nephew and tell him his uncle was alive and well and not to worry. He thanked us over and over again for coming to untie him, and then we left.

Down by the old spring where Dragonfly and I had gone for water, we all lay down one at a time and drank, horse fashion. Then we turned around and looked back up at the cabin with the blue smoke rising slowly up out of the chimney and with the old man standing in the doorway, his long, white whiskers shining in the afternoon sun. All of a sudden he lifted his hand and waved good-bye to us—No, he had both hands raised, like one of the pictures in my Bible story book where an old prophet was raising his hands to bless somebody. For a minute I thought of the funny cloud I'd seen the other night which looked like an old man with long gold whiskers reaching down to his waist.

Then we started down the hill toward home, not forgetting to stop at the swimming hole for a good swim so we could tell our folks we wouldn't need a bath tonight, this being Saturday and all boys having to take a bath on Saturday night whether they want to or not. Some of us had to take them even oftener than that.

12

DID I TELL YOU that we nearly always went to town
on Saturday nights? We had to, you know, to buy gro-
ceries and things. So when we were dressed, Dad called
and soon we were driving along in his car toward
town, which was about five miles away.

"Now, don't you get into any mischief!" Dad said
to me when we stopped in front of the big spraying
fountain on the main street of our town and I slid
out of the car and ran over to where Poetry and Dragonfly were waiting for me.

"Hello, Bill," they said.

"Hello, Dragonfly. Hello, Poetry." They were both
wearing their Sunday clothes. We stood watching the
water spraying down from above and falling into a
big cement pool right in front of us with electric
lights shining down on it from lampposts all around
it. You could see maybe a dozen goldfish swimming
around in the pool. Say, with water splashing and the
band playing up the street and hundreds of people
standing around talking and laughing and especially
with Poetry and Dragonfly there, all of us liking each
other a lot, it seemed good to be alive.

"I wonder if it's deep enough to swim in," Poetry
said. I was thinking the same thing, and so was

Dragonfly. And do you know we had to go away and quit watching that fountain because it made us want to go swimming so bad it made us feel sad all over!

We started walking along Main Street with Poetry in the middle and with Dragonfly and me on each side of him when all of a sudden Dragonfly said, "Psst!" just like he always does when he's seen or heard something important. So we stopped quick to find out what it was.

"It's Circus' dad!" he said. "See him walking crazy-like? I bet he's drunk!" And sure enough, he was.

"I hope he hasn't got a gun," I said, remembering he was always carrying one when he went hunting and was an awful good shot.

He kept shuffling along, reaching out with each foot like he was having trouble finding the sidewalk.

"Let's follow him to see where he goes," Poetry said, and we did. Pretty soon he staggered up to a place where they sell beer and kinda fell against the door. Then he pushed it open and went inside. We stood there looking in through the smoky glass door panel and saw him lean up against the bar, throw down some money, and say something to the bartender. It was disgusting to see him drink like that and it made me mad all over to see that big, fat-stomached bartender take the money and give him another glass of beer when I knew Circus' folks were poor and needed all the money they could get for food and clothes and things. We were glad Little Jim wasn't with us 'cause he would have felt so bad about it. He liked Circus so well he wouldn't have had any fun at all. As it was, it kinda took away the good taste of the bag of peanuts we were eating right that minute.

Well, we went on walking around feeling kinda sad when pretty soon we saw Circus himself sitting alone on a bench in front of an empty store building looking like he'd lost his best friend.

"Hello, Circus," I said, and Poetry and Dragonfly said the same thing. We offered him some of our peanuts and sat down beside him.

"What's the matter?" I asked. But he didn't answer. He just kept sitting there looking sad not even taking any of our peanuts. I noticed he didn't have on nearly as nice clothes as the rest of us, but they were clean and neat. His shoes were old, too, but he had them pretty well blacked, and they looked all right. He had a very good mother.

"Wait a minute," Dragonfly said, and he got up and ran down the street and came back with a big bag of fresh popcorn, knowing Circus liked popcorn better than anything. But he didn't take any, and we didn't try very hard to make him. We all sat there feeling sad, none of us saying anything for a long time.

Pretty soon Circus said, "Dad's drunk again." Then he sighed and took some of my peanuts and Dragonfly's popcorn. Down the street the band was playing a beautiful number, "The Stars and Stripes Forever." People were walking past in front of us, going both ways, talking and laughing. Everybody seemed happy except us.

"That's a pretty band piece," Circus said. "I always wanted to play in a band. Maybe someday I'll run away from home and get a job and make enough money to buy a cornet."

"Doesn't your mother like you any more?" Dragonfly asked.

Circus kinda choked on the popcorn he had in his mouth and coughed a little. Then he said, "Maybe if I ran away and got some work, I could send her the money I made."

Just then Circus' dad came shuffling down the street laughing like a crazy man. In a jiffy Circus was out of his seat and running down an alley as fast as he could go with us right after him. I thought maybe he was going to run away right now, and I didn't want him to 'cause I knew how his mother would feel. In the alley about a block from the main street we stopped behind somebody's garage where there wasn't any light and listened for a minute to see if anybody was coming. Nobody was.

"He's mad at me," Circus said, " 'cause I went into the beer parlor about a half hour ago and told him to stop drinking or I'd tell Mother. He'll give me a terrible lickin' if he catches me."

Right beside us was a telephone pole, and I couldn't help but think how, if Circus was happy, he'd probably be halfway up to the top of it by now. There was the brightest, roundest moon up in the sky you ever saw and if Poetry'd been happy, he'd probably have started to say:

"Hey, diddle, diddle,
  The cat and the fiddle,
  The cow jumped over the moon;
    The little dog laughed to see such sport,
    And the dish ran away with the spoon."

We stayed there in the shadow of that little garage for maybe five minutes, thinking and saying different things. I was wishing Circus was my brother so he could have my dad for his daddy when all of a sudden we heard footsteps coming down the alley. We crowded down behind a big box there and waited. And would you believe it? In a minute two men stopped there in the dark, and one of them was my dad and the other was Circus'. Say, you can guess we had a hard time keeping still, and I can't tell you how queer I felt inside.

"You're making a big fool out of yourself!" my dad said disgustedly to Circus' dad.

Circus' dad swore terribly and said, "I don't want any more kids! Three girls and one good-for-nothing boy is enough!"

Say, my fists doubled up when he said that 'cause I knew he was talking about Circus and I reckon maybe it isn't wrong to get mad at something like that either.

I peeped out from behind the box, and I could see my dad standing there tall and straight in the moonlight looking so clean and good. Circus' dad was standing all slouched over with his hat on crooked and some of his mussed-up hair sticking out on one side. His tie was twisted, and his face, what I could see of it, looked terrible. For a minute I remembered what Big Jim had said that afternoon about sin, quoting from the Bible, saying, "Be not deceived; God is not mocked!" I decided nobody could fool God. It was like my dad had just said, Circus' dad was making a big fool out of himself.

"Now you listen, Dan Browne!" my dad said roughly, "you're not drinking another drop tonight, do you hear?"

"'Snone of your business!" Circus' dad grumbled back and swore again. "It's my money and I'll spend it like I please. Anyway, when a new baby comes to my house I've got a right to celebrate."

But say, my dad was getting angry too—with the right kind of anger. He just reached out his big strong hands, grabbed Circus' dad by the shoulder, shook him like a big dog shakes a rat, and said roughly, "You ought to celebrate by getting down on your knees, Dan Browne, and praying to God almighty that He'll forgive your sins and make you man enough to be a good father to your children and a decent husband to your wife. Mrs. Browne is one of the grandest little women that ever drew breath, and

97

your boy is one of the finest boys in the country. And you—You're just a good-for-nothing *drunk!* Shame on you, Dan Browne!"

And that's how we came to learn that Circus had a new baby at their house too. Well, my dad wouldn't let Circus' dad go home that night 'cause he knew he'd cause all kinds of trouble and maybe do something terrible. So he hunted up the town marshal, which is the same as a policeman, and they locked him up in jail, which is where he belonged.

Also, that's how Circus came to stay all night at my house. With the new baby coming to their house, there might be a lot of excitement. Big Jim's mother was staying there too to help take care of the baby, so there wouldn't be beds enough, although as Circus said, he would just as leave sleep in the barn, as he'd done it before when his dad was mad at him about something. Anyway, they wouldn't want a noisy boy around right away.

My dad drove all the way to Circus' house to tell them that Circus was going to sleep with me that night, his folks not having a telephone 'cause his dad used all the money for whiskey and beer. Then Dad stopped at Big Jim's house and made arrangements for somebody to do the chores at Circus' the next morning, Big Jim living right across the road from them anyway, as I told you before.

13

WHEN WE GOT BACK to my house, it was after ten o'clock, more than an hour past the time I usually went to bed in the summer.

Charlotte Ann was wide awake when we came in and was making a terrible noise, crying like everything. Circus and I went in for a minute to see what all the fuss was about. And say, that little thing stopped crying the minute we came in. Or I should have said, the minute she saw Circus!

"I know how to look at girls," he said to me, grinning. "I've got three sisters."

"Four," I said. "You're getting a new one at your house tonight." And he said, "Yeah, that's right," kinda disappointed.

"Good night," I called to my mother in the other room. Then I looked at Miss Trillium, the nurse, with pretty crimson cheeks and blue eyes and said good night again, special. She was holding a bottle with a nipple on it for Charlotte Ann who was on her lap, and she looked up and smiled at me and said, "Good night, Bill."

Circus said good night too, and she gave him a nice smile but not nearly as nice as the one she'd given me, I thought. Then Circus and I went upstairs, after watching Charlotte Ann drink her milk for a minute. Say, she was the cutest little thing! Even Circus looked at her like he thought so too, and I got to thinking maybe he liked his sisters better'n he let on. Most boys don't want to let anybody know they like girls at all, even when they do.

Well, it didn't take us long to get undressed and ready for bed. Circus didn't seem very happy and you couldn't blame him with his dad drunk and in jail. But in spite of that, he felt sorry for his dad. "He's good to us sometimes, though," he said while we were undressing. "One day last week he told Mom he'd never get drunk again in his life, and I saw him give her a big hug like he really meant it. And Mom cried 'cause she was so happy. But those old newspapers and magazines Dad reads have great big whiskey advertisements in them with important-looking men drinking and saying how good it is. And the first thing you know Dad goes to town and buys some again."

"You know what I wish?" Circus said, and I could see he was getting mad at the people who made whiskey and sold it and advertised it. "I wish," he said with his fists doubled up and his voice trembly, "I wish they'd just *once* take a picture of my dad when he's drunk and looking like he did uptown tonight and put *that* in their old papers and magazines! I bet *that* wouldn't make anybody want to buy any!"

Circus kept his fists doubled up and looked so fierce for a minute it almost scared me. But I was kinda proud of him that he could get mad at something like that 'cause it's all right to get angry at sin. My dad says so; and once even Jesus was angry at some people in the Bible who were doing wrong. And I guess maybe God hates sin terribly!

Pretty soon we were in bed with the lamp out and the moonlight shining on us. Then all of a sudden I remembered I hadn't said my prayers. In fact, I'd been thinking about it quite a little while and didn't know what to do about it. I was sure Circus had never said his prayers in his life 'cause even if he did have a good mother, she wasn't a Christian yet. And she'd never taught him to pray.

So I began to think that maybe I'd say my prayers in bed. But I remembered the story we'd read in school when we were in the fourth grade about "Little Arthur's Prayer" and how that brave little fellow had knelt down before a whole roomful of boys and prayed before going to bed. So I lay thinking, wondering if Circus'd make fun of me. Then I began to think about what Little Jim would do if he were here, and I knew that that little fellow wouldn't even think about being afraid or ashamed. So pretty soon I decided on something, and say, talk about being brave in a fight or something! I guess I never had any harder time in my life being brave than right that minute. My heart started beating awful fast and I was actually scared to do what I knew I had to do.

I asked Circus if he remembered "Little Arthur's

Prayer," and he did. Then I told him about Poetry praying every night before he went to bed. I knew he liked Poetry a lot, so pretty soon I said suddenly, with my heart still beating fast, "Let's us do it too," not telling him I always did it every night anyway, although I guess maybe I should have.

Circus kinda grunted, and then said, "You do it first."

Well, in a jiffy I was out of bed and saying my prayers quietly, like I did sometimes anyway, knowing Jesus could hear me even if I didn't talk loud. I prayed for Circus' dad there in jail and for his mother and for his new baby sister. Then I jumped up off my knees with my heart as light as a feather and said, "I guess I feel better now." Then I climbed into bed over on the other side of Circus.

Circus lay there for about a half minute, and in a jiffy there he was down on his knees right where I'd been, his pretty brown hair shining in the moonlight. I guess I never did tell you Circus had the prettiest brown hair anybody ever saw.

And do you know? He had never prayed before in his whole life and I never thought about him not knowing what to say. And all in a jiffy he was through. He jumped up real quick like and said the same thing I'd said when I got up, "I guess I feel better now," and jumped into bed with his face turned the other way on his pillow.

After awhile I said to Circus, "I prayed for your

dad." He didn't say anything. I wouldn't have found out how terribly bad he felt about his dad if I hadn't kinda put my arm around him like the boys do when they like each other a lot and felt a teeny weeny wet spot on his pillow like maybe a tear or something had dropped there. But I didn't tell him I'd felt it. I just rolled over and said, "Good night." Pretty soon it was morning again, just like it was in Poetry's tent.

And from that night on, Circus said his prayers every night. The next time I saw Little Jim I told him about it, and he was so tickled he actually turned a somersault just like Circus does. There was a little tree right close, and he climbed up it about as quick as Circus could have done it.

14

WHEN CIRCUS AND I woke up the next morning, the sun was already shining into our window making a big yellow square on the green wall paper just above the foot of the bed.

We lay there for a minute before getting up, and I was looking at the sunlight when all of a sudden there was a little shadow moving around in it. I knew in a jiffy that it was a bird sitting on our windowsill, a sparrow maybe, preening his feathers and making funny little bird noises. His little head with its sharp little bill kept bobbing around kinda crazy-like, just like the bobber on my fishing line had done that day last week when I'd caught that big black bass. Ho, hum! I wished it had been two feet long. Say, that week was the most exciting week of my whole life, I reckon. Anyway, up to now, I thought.

Circus let out a big loud yawn that scared the bird and it flew away. And just that minute Charlotte Ann started in crying downstairs.

"See there!" I said to Circus, sitting up in bed and pretending to be angry, "you woke her up!"

But he just grinned at me and said, "I'll run downstairs and let her look at me, and she'll stop crying right away." He rolled out of bed and started dressing. Both of us dressed in about two jiffies, me putting on overalls so I could help dad with the chores, that is, if they weren't already done. Then we went tumbling downstairs and out of doors feeling like two frisky young colts. Just that minute Circus saw our big high grape arbor with a cross piece at the top. Right there where there weren't any vines was a good place to do athletic stunts. Quicker'n anything he was right up on it "skinning the cat" and hanging by his legs and everything.

"Hey!" I cried to him, "you'll get your good clothes all wrinkled and dirty!"

He looked at me surprised-like, his face looking awful funny upside down, for he was still hanging by his legs. His brown hair was all tangled up on top of his head.

He got down right quick and said, "That's right! I have to be careful!" And he really meant it. But we had so many things for a boy to climb upon, such as the big cherry tree in our yard, the high rope swing in our walnut tree and the ladder leading up into the haymow in our barn, that I had to take Circus back upstairs to my room and get a pair of overalls for him or his clothes wouldn't have been fit to wear to Sunday school at all. You see, I'd made up my mind he was going to Sunday school with me.

"I won't go to Sunday school with you," he said. "My clothes aren't good enough for that." And he looked kinda sad again. Maybe he happened to think about his dad in jail. I don't know, for he didn't act like Circus after that, and I felt very sorry for him.

"Besides," he said, "people will look at me and won't like me 'cause my dad's in jail. Anyway I haven't been to Sunday school since I was little."

Well, just then my dad came out of the barn with two big pails of milk, each one with about an inch of rich, yellow foam on top of it.

"Why didn't you wake me up?" I said to Dad, feeling guilty 'cause I hadn't helped him.

But Dad just laughed and said, "You don't have company every day, so I decided to let you sleep." I thought that was pretty nice of him, don't you? Even if I didn't like to work, I liked to help my dad get the work done 'cause it's only good-for-nothing boys that won't help their parents without being scolded or whipped or something.

After breakfast Circus and I helped with the dishes. He did it awkward-like 'cause he had three sisters and didn't ever have to help at home. And who do you suppose *washed* those dishes? You'd never guess in the world, but my dad did! You should have seen him with Mom's apron on looking just like a woman, unless you saw his big brown arms with the sleeves rolled up and his moustache and his reddish-brown hair, Mom's hair being almost black with little gray streaks in it. Maybe it might seem funny to some people to see a man washing dishes and boys wiping them. But say when there's a swell new baby come to live at your house, you'd be willing to do most anything to help take care of her. It's that important.

Pretty soon it was time to go to Sunday school and Circus still hadn't made up his mind to go, but we all told him his clothes looked good enough, and Dad gave him a brand new necktie to wear, saying he had too many now. I noticed especially that it was the one I'd given Dad for his birthday two months ago, but I didn't say anything, being glad to let Circus have it. Just to keep him from feeling too embarrassed, I put on my second best shoes instead of my best. And since he didn't have a good cap, we both went bareheaded. "Besides," I told him, "I'll bet Jesus didn't have a lot of fancy clothes to wear when He was a little boy 'cause His folks were poor."

"Were they?" he asked, surprised.

"Sure," I said, "and when He grew up He didn't even have a nice home to live in, nor any money to pay taxes with. Why one time He sent Peter down to the brook with his fishing pole and hook and told him he'd find the money to pay their taxes right in the fish's mouth." I explained that Jesus was trying to teach Peter that when he became a preacher later on the people who got saved under his sermons would take care of him. Peter started in fishing for men not long after that, you know.

But Circus, not having heard the Bible explained

very much, didn't quite understand what I was talking about.

"Is *that* in the Bible?" he asked. We were standing up in our big high swing just then, facing each other and pumping ourselves higher and higher.

"Sure it is!" I said. "There's some of the best stories in the world right in the Bible."

"Do you suppose there'll be any jails in heaven?" he asked.

We were swinging awful high right then, back and forth, the cool air blowing against our faces, our shirt sleeves flapping in the wind, our hair getting all mussed up and would have to be combed again before we could go to church.

"Jails!" I said, trying to remember something I'd heard our minister say. "No, I don't think so. What would God want jails up there for!"

Circus didn't say anything for a minute. Then he asked, "What'll He do with people that get drunk and kill people and things like that?"

You know, I'd never thought about that before. "I don't know," I said, thinking I'd ask my dad or mom or Little Jim or somebody as soon as I got a chance. Then I happened to think of something important, and I didn't know whether it was right or not but I asked Little Jim the next day, and he said it was: "I think maybe all the people who aren't saved won't even get into heaven at all but will have to go to—to some terrible—*jail!*" I said to Circus.

He looked awful sad for a minute and we both forgot to pump and our swing almost stopped. "You mean—*hell?*" he asked.

And that's how I began to wonder whether I was saved myself or not. I knew I wasn't a drunkard like Circus' dad or a bank robber or anything like that, but I felt right down in my heart that I needed Jesus anyway. For if people didn't need Him why did He come down here from heaven to die for them?

But I didn't tell Circus how I felt just then nor my dad nor anybody. But I thought maybe sometime I'd tell Little Jim, and I might even tell Jesus Himself the next time I prayed.

Well, pretty soon it was time to go to Sunday school, and away we went in Dad's car, stopping at Poetry's house for him and at Dragonfly's for him. Big Jim and Little Jim were waiting for us in front of the church when we got there.

We had the nicest teacher for our class. She knew all about boys and you could tell by the way she looked at us that she liked us, and wouldn't get angry if we forgot to listen for a minute or maybe whispered or something. It was especially hard for Poetry to be good either in church or in school on account of his being so mischievous and not able to help it. But even a mischievous boy can be good if he wants to.

The only thing wrong with going to Sunday school on a hot day is that you have to wear shoes, and you keep wanting to take them off and go running lickety-sizzle through the woods or go swimming or fishing or something. And if your teacher doesn't understand boys, it's still harder.

Well, right after Sunday school we all went out doors a minute for some fresh air before the bell rang for church to begin. Then we went back inside. Every one of us stayed for church too. Big Jim had given a talk about that once. You see, one time last year when there'd been a fire in our church, we all went to a Sunday school in town. Right after Sunday school was over, almost half of the other boys and girls went home not even staying for church! Big Jim was disgusted and Little Jim thought it was terrible. *Think* of it. Not staying for church service. Shucks! Didn't those kids' parents *know* anything! Didn't they know that if you don't want a boy to grow up to be no good at all and maybe a gangster or something, he's got to go to Sunday school and church when he's little? Anybody ought to know *that!*

Well, when my dad saw all of us boys sitting there in a row all by ourselves, with Poetry and me sitting side by side, he gave me a look with his big eyebrows down that said, "Now then, William Jasper Collins! You see to it that you don't get into mischief!"

Maybe our pastor wasn't the most wonderful speaker in the world, and I coudn't understand *everything* he said, but he always had something in his sermon that a boy could understand. And that made it interesting. I guess he remembered when he was a boy and couldn't understand everything either, unless it was explained in boy language. Anyway, his sermons helped you to love Jesus a little more; and when he told an interesting story to explain some Bible verse, I always sat up and listened even if I had been wiggling around a little bit before that.

Well, the music started and we were all singing away. Poetry growled along trying to sing bass, but he couldn't because his voice was just half soprano and half something else, when somebody's baby started to cry and I forgot all about that song and everything for thinking of Charlotte Ann. Say, I looked at Circus, and he looked at me. And then he looked at the baby just like he had done at Charlotte Ann last night, but it didn't do a bit of good. In fact, the baby cried even louder than before! And for a minute I had a hard time to keep from laughing. But pretty soon they took the baby out, like you're supposed to do when they won't quit crying in church, and everything was all right.

They finished the song and were starting another when all of a sudden the door opened and somebody came in and started walking down the aisle toward the front of the church. And would you believe it? It was Old Man Paddler himself, his long white hair combed nice and neat. He had a good suit of clothes on and he was walking pretty spry for such an old man, looking just like Moses or somebody.

I tell you we all sat up and took notice, and for a

minute the singing almost stopped. Little Jim's mother, who was playing the piano, turned halfway around and actually struck some of the wrong keys for a minute.

Our minister must have known him, for after looking surprised a minute, he came right down off the platform and went to him and shook hands with him, smiling all over like he was his very best friend. Then he whispered something in the old man's ear like he was asking a question, and I saw that old head nod like he was saying yes. Then we went on singing.

Well, pretty soon I knew what our minister had asked him, for when we'd finished the song and we'd finished reading some verses out of the Bible, he said: "I'm sure we are happy to have one of our charter members with us this morning, after a trip around the world, one whom many of you have known and loved. At this time we shall be led in prayer by Seneth Paddler."

Well, that old man just lifted his fine old gray head toward the ceiling with his face looking up, only his eyes were shut. And his kind old voice started in praying, trembling along like it wasn't very strong and might break any time. I shut my eyes like you're supposed to when anybody prays, and for a minute it was almost scary in that church 'cause it kinda seemed like heaven had moved right down to earth. I actually had to open my eyes to be sure it wasn't so. And say, that old man's white forehead was shining and his long whiskers looked awful pretty. I actually kept my eyes open almost all the rest of the way through that prayer, forgetting to close them.

And do you know what? It's a secret and I never told anybody before, but just as Old Man Paddler was finishing his prayer, I shut my eyes real quick and told Jesus I loved Him, and asked Him to come into my heart for sure so I'd know whether I was saved or not. Then I prayed real quick for Circus' dad, and got done at the same time Old Man Paddler did.

And do you know what else? It kinda seemed from that minute on that Jesus and I had a secret. It seemed that I was an honest to goodness Christian, and that some day Circus' dad would be saved and wouldn't get drunk any more, and Circus wouldn't have to run away 'cause his dad would be good to him, and Circus could have a cornet and play in the band, and his mother would be happy, and they'd all go to church like families are supposed to.

The meeting was over and we went home, Circus riding home with Big Jim and his folks.

After dinner was over at our house, I saw Dad get his big black Bible and go out to the car. I knew he was going to town to the jail and talk to Circus' dad. So I ran down to the barn and climbed up into our haymow and went away back up in the hay where nobody could see me, or even hear me, and got down on both of my knees and told Jesus about our secret. I asked Him to help Dad and to make that part of the secret about Circus' dad come true just as quick as He could. Then to make it seem like a bargain I just stuck my little New Testament there in a crack in a log and left it. You see, I still had it in my pocket from carrying it to Sunday school. And all of a sudden I began to be awful happy because it seemed like Jesus had forgiven all my sins and that He had really and truly saved me. I even cried a little bit all by myself and I didn't care if I did. I loved Jesus so much inside that it seemed my heart would burst.

Then I climbed down out of the haymow and there at the bottom of the ladder was old Mixy, our black and white cat, and I felt so good I just scooped her up in my arms and hugged her and yelled, "Whoopee!"

But say, Mixy didn't seem to appreciate the fact that I was happy, for she got scared when I yelled, "Whoopee!" She scrambled out of my arms and went lickety-sizzle across the floor and crawled into a hole that leads under the barn. Then I went up to the house to see Charlotte Ann and maybe do a little errand or something for Miss Trillium, if she wanted me to, and to wait for Dragonfly who had promised to come over to play with me that afternoon.

15

CHARLOTTE ANN still wasn't very cheerful, nothing like she was a week or two later when she'd gotten used to living in this world and maybe had decided that my red hair and freckles weren't anything to be afraid of. Say, she didn't need to act so disgusted with my red hair! 'Cause when you got a look at her black curls up real close, they looked like maybe they'd be dark red themselves some day. But then, of course, she didn't know that. Babies don't know anything, in fact; *nearly* all babies don't, except Charlotte Ann.

I stood there beside Mom's bed where she was resting, and I looked at the golden fawn lilies I'd picked, with the blue and purple violets mixed up with them. "Do you think she liked them?" I asked Mom. You know, I was getting awful lonesome for my mom, and I tell you it wasn't going to be easy to let Charlotte Ann have all the attention around the house. Why, my dad was just crazy about that little thing! Watching him, if you didn't happen to notice how big he was, or see his moustache, you couldn't tell him from Circus, for he'd almost stand on his head in front of Charlotte Ann just to get her to smile at him. And he'd make the funniest faces! It was almost disgusting to see him make over her like that. That is, it was until one day I caught myself doing the same thing, and then it didn't seem so bad. But that's getting pretty far ahead of my story 'cause little Charlotte Ann didn't even know enough to smile until she was several weeks old.

Well, I kept waiting for Dragonfly to come, wondering why he was so late, when pretty soon I saw him running up the road just as fast he could. He opened our gate quick and hurried up to the house. I ran out to meet him.

Well, after taking a long walk, we'd had a drink at the spring, and then we took turns looking at different things with my binoculars. Pretty soon Dragonfly whispered, "Psst! Come here, Bill! Let's watch this spider eat her dinner!"

He was standing looking down into a big hollow stump that was big enough for Poetry to stand in, and he had his finger up to his lips.

"I don't see any spider," I said, peeping in, both of us standing so our shadows wouldn't fall on the stump, although I did see a nice new spider web stretched across one corner.

"Just wait," he said, and he showed me a fly he'd caught and was holding by its wings. He broke off one wing so it couldn't fly. Then he dropped the fly right into the middle of that sticky web, where it began to kick and squirm and get all tangled up. All spider webs are sticky, you know. Say, that web bounced around and shook almost as much as Poetry's bed does when he turns over in his sleep.

"Psst!" Dragonfly said. And in a jiffy we saw coming out of her hiding place a little black spider, hurrying toward that fly.

"She's coming backwards," I said, and sure enough she was. We couldn't see very well 'cause we couldn't get close enough to look at her with the magnifying glass without scaring her away, and the binoculars wouldn't help either. She was one of the smallest black spiders you ever saw, with kinda long legs, yet not very long either.

Suddenly Dragonfly let out a gasp and jumped back so quick he bumped into me and almost knocked me down.

"What's the matter?" I said, not seeing anything to be so excited about.

"I—I *saw* it!" he exclaimed. "That reddish mark on her underneath side! She's a—a *black widow spider!*"

I tell you Dragonfly was excited, and as I said once before, getting excited is contagious. For a minute I was almost scared, although I knew we couldn't have been bitten unless we'd been closer than we were.

You see, the black widow spider is a little black spider with a reddish mark on its stomach, shaped kinda like an hour glass or else like a couple of triangles. It's the most dangerous spider in the world, but there aren't very many of them, so boys don't need

117

to be afraid of finding one all the time. Of course, it's a good thing to kill any spider you see around the house or cellar or anywhere, especially black ones.

Well, we got a couple of wide sticks and sneaked back to watch a minute. And already that fly was fastened so tight in the web it couldn't have gotten away even if it had wings. Black widow spiders, you know, give off some kind of fluid that dries almost as quick as rubber cement like the kind my dad uses to patch his automobile tires, and no fly or bug could get away even if it tried terribly hard.

In a jiffy that spider ran up to the fly like she was terribly mad at it and she must have bitten it for it started kicking and shaking harder than ever.

"It's dying!" Dragonfly said. "She's killed it!"

And sure enough! In a minute that fly was quiet and Mrs. Spider was busy sucking on it kinda like she was sucking water through a straw.

"What'll we do?" Dragonfly said. "If it's a real black widow, it ought to be killed."

"It's the first one I ever saw," I said.

"And maybe the last one, although sometimes there are several together—especially if she's laid any eggs and they're hatched."

It would have been silly to have poked around in that stump with our sticks trying to kill that spider, or we might have gotten bit ourselves.

My dad says if anybody gets bit by a black widow spider, it might not even hurt at all at first, but pretty soon it will. And after awhile you get sick at your stomach like you didn't want your dinner. And all your muscles down below your stomach get all tight and hard and you start sweating all over and maybe having a chill, and your skin starts to burn.

But if you get bit by one, you ought to have iodine put on the bite real quick and have somebody get a good doctor as soon as you can—awful soon, in fact. And be sure to tell him exactly what happened so he'll know what to do for you.

Well, while we were standing there trying to decide what to do, we heard somebody coming and we looked up just in time to see a man dodging behind a tree like he was afraid somebody'd see him.

Quick as anything, we darted behind some bushes and dropped down in the grass, wondering if it was some of the gang trying to sneak up on us.

Dragonfly had my binoculars, and pretty soon he saw who it was. I guess my red hair must have stood right up on end for a minute when he told me.

"It's the robber!" he whispered, trying to be calm like Big Jim and to think what to do. "He must have gotten out of jail somehow and is running away," he said. "Maybe he's trying to hide down along the swamp again."

"Let's run!" I said, and in a jiffy we were on our way as fast as we could go, and we didn't stop until we had climbed clear up on top of the big hill where our gang meets sometimes. There we lay down be-

119

hind the big rocks to get our wind, thinking maybe we'd better go on home quick and telephone for the sheriff again. Just that minute we thought we heard a car stop up on the road not far from my house, and we decided maybe the sheriff and his posse were already there. I got my binoculars up to my eyes and looked quick but didn't see anybody, and then I looked down toward the spring just in time to see somebody come from behind a tree and go straight toward that old stump where we'd been not more than ten minutes ago.

Say, that man stopped right behind that old stump for a minute, and Dragonfly nudged me and said, "What do you suppose he's doing there?"

"I don't know," I said, thinking what if he climbed inside.

Just that minute the man stood up real quick with his head showing just above the top of the stump, like he was looking for something. But he seemed to be having a hard time finding what he wanted, and all the time we were scared he'd get bit by the spider. We couldn't see very well, but it looked like the man had a gun too, and he had climbed right up on top of the stump and was looking down inside.

All of a sudden Dragonfly couldn't keep still any longer for even if it was a robber we didn't want him to get bit. So Dragonfly screamed like he was scared himself, and his scream was so loud and frightening that the man looked up quick, then his foot slipped or something and he fell down inside. Or else he jumped in to hide. We couldn't tell which.

I tell you I felt creepy all over, for I realized what might happen to him if that was a sure enough black widow spider. But I knew the man had a gun and that he was a desperate criminal and might shoot anybody if he thought they were after him. And do you know? As much as I wanted him to be caught and knowing how wicked he was and everything, still I began to feel sorry for him. I kept thinking about what Little Jim would say and how he would feel if the man got bit and had to die without letting Jesus into his heart.

"Let's go home quick!" I said to Dragonfly.

"Why?"

"Cause I'm going to telephone for a doctor!"

"A doctor! What for?"

"Why, if he gets bit by that spider, and we don't get a doctor for him, he'll die!" Already I was running as fast as I could toward our house, with Dragonfly right at my heels.

I didn't even take time to open our front gate which opens kinda hard anyway. I climbed over quick and ran up the walk, burst open the front door without knocking, and grabbed the telephone. In a jiffy I was talking to Dr. Gordon, our family doctor, with Mom and the nurse looking at me like they thought I was crazy and telling me to keep still or I'd wake up Charlotte Ann.

121

"Quick, Doctor!" I said into the telephone, "This is Bill Collins! Come out here quick and bring some iodine and whatever you need for a man who's been bit by a black widow spider!"

Then I hung up.

16

IN ABOUT TWENTY MINUTES the doctor came, bringing another doctor with him. My dad had come home in the meantime. Then we all went down through the woods toward the old hollow stump, and there we found the man lying on the grass. He was all doubled up and trying to vomit, and he was sweating terribly. Right on his forehead—in fact, just above his left eye —was a swollen place about twice as big as a mosquito bite with two little red spots on it.

I guess I never was so surprised in my life when I saw who it was; for it wasn't the bank robber at all. But would you believe it? *It was Circus' dad!* And lying right beside him were three great big whiskey bottles and his gun. You know, I told you before Circus' dad was an awful good shot and he was always carrying a gun.

"Why, it's Dan Browne!" my dad cried. "I just took him home about an hour ago!"

Circus' dad rolled over and groaned with his arms and shoulders twitching. Then he saw my dad and looked scared for a minute, and between groans he said to him, "Honest, Mr. Collins! I wasn't going to

—drink—it! I—had these bottles hid—here—and —and I came down to get them. . . . I was goin' to put them up—on the stump and—and shoot 'em." Then Circus' dad rolled over and groaned, still trying to vomit, and staying all doubled up like he had the cramps something terrible. *"Spider!"* he cried, pointing toward the stump. *"Don't let the boys g-get b-bit!"*

It didn't take the doctors long to put iodine on those little red spots to keep him from getting what they call "secondary infection."

For a minute those doctors stood there talking while Dragonfly and I watched and listened. And we heard a lot of long words which I didn't understand at the time, but which I've since learned how to spell and pronounce 'cause maybe some day I'm going to be a doctor myself.

The doctors decided to use a hypodermic and inject some *magnesium sulphate* right into one of his veins.

They took him to the hospital as quick as they could, being careful to keep him as quiet as possible. In the hospital they gave him another shot in the muscles of his arm, of some kind of serum—"convalescent serum," I think my dad said it was—which is made from blood of somebody who's been bit by a black widow spider and got well.

Along about five o'clock in the afternoon, my dad came home, for he'd gone to the hospital with them, and I ran out to the car to meet him.

Dad just sat there under the steering wheel for a while, not saying anything, so I climbed in beside him, Dragonfly having gone home about a half hour before.

Then my dad kinda put his arm over the back of the car seat and let it touch my shoulders like he was not only my dad and I was his boy, but like we were real good friends. It felt good to have my dad do that, so I just sat there thinking and wondering whether Circus' dad was going to live or not and wishing I'd tell Dad I now knew for sure that I was saved.

"Well, Bill," Dad said, and that made me feel better. Then he said, "Your quick action and presence of mind saved a life this afternoon."

I felt proud to have him say that, but it didn't seem as important as something else just then, so I said, "Is —is Circus' dad saved yet?"

Say, my dad looked at me quick to see if I meant it, and I could feel his fingers tighten a little around my shoulder as if he liked me even better.

"No," he said. "I talked to him a long time at the jail and he promised to live better and to be kind to his family and not get drunk any more, but he would not accept Jesus into his heart."

"It'll be hard for him to be good without Jesus helping him, won't it?" I asked.

"Too hard," Dad said, "but he'll be in the hospital maybe a week and he'll have time to think and pray and read the Bible."

After a while when Dad and I were doing the chores and I was up in the haymow throwing down some hay for the cows and horses, I climbed away up into the corner again and took my little New Testament out and turned to one of the verses which my Mom had had me learn when I was little. I read it again just to be sure it really said it and just to be sure I could know for sure I was a Christian and was saved. This is what it said, "For God so loved the world, that he gave his only begotten Son, that whosoever believeth in him should not perish, but have everlasting life." And I *knew* I was saved 'cause it says if I *believe* in Him (meaning with all my heart, of course) then I *have* everlasting life, and I wouldn't *have* to wait till I died to be sure I was going to heaven. I guess there isn't anything more wonderful than that, is there?

Then I got down on my knees and shut my eyes and said, "Dear Lord Jesus, I thank You for saving me and making me so happy and for giving me such a nice little baby sister. And please help me to act like a Christian so other people will want to be saved too. And please save Circus' dad and help him to see how much he needs You. And bless Little Jim and Poetry and Big Jim and Circus and Dragonfly and—and all the boys in the world."

I got up from my knees and put my New Testament back in the log again and started whistling and throwing down more hay, and I decided to leave my Bible there until Circus' dad was saved.

126

The next day some men came out from town and poured kerosene over that old hollow stump and on the inside of it, and set fire to it, so if there were any other black widow spiders there, or any eggs, they'd all be burned up. And do you know, we never did find any more of them in our neighborhood, even though we watched carefully for years.

But here I am, getting to the end of my story and I haven't even told you about the time, about a month later, when Little Jim killed the black bear and maybe saved all of us from getting hurt. But it'd make this story too long to write here. Maybe if I have time, I'll tell you about it someday and a lot of other interesting things about the Sugar Creek Gang and Old Man Paddler, and how Circus got his cornet, and how Little Charlotte Ann grew and everything.

Anyway, the gang was all there while the men were burning that old stump. We were lying there in the tall grass not far from the creek talking and laughing and having a good time watching the big yellow flames eat up that stump just like a hungry boy eating a big plateful of raw fried potatoes, or licking a lollipop or something.

Even Circus seemed happy 'cause he knew his dad was going to get well. Pretty soon he jumped up and started climbing a little tree right behind us, and in a jiffy he was perched up on a limb, grinning like a monkey and looking like the same happy old Circus again.

And while those flames leaped higher and higher and the blue and purple smoke rolled up in little cloud waves toward the sky, Poetry started quoting "America the Beautiful," saying:

> "Oh beautiful, for spacious skies,
> For amber waves of grain,
> For purple mountain majesties
> Above the fruited plain . . ."

Just then an old shitepoke went flying up the creek with its long ugly neck sticking out in front of it like the long tongue on my green coaster wagon. I got out my binoculars and watched it until it disappeared. Pretty soon we thought we'd watched the fire long enough, so we all jumped up and went down to the old swimming hole and went in swimming.

Moody Press, a ministry of the Moody Bible Institute, is designed for education, evangelization and edification. If we may assist you in knowing more about Christ and the Christian life, please write us without obligation to: Moody Press, c/o MLM, Chicago, Illinois 60610.